A V  Y

WHAT a DRAGON
Desires
STAR OF THE NORTH DRAGONS

"What a Dragon Desires"

written by Ava Cuvay

Copyright ©2024

Published by Drinking the Stars Press, LLC

Cover Design by Fiona Jayde Media

Copy Edited by Nan Reinhardt

ISBN # 979-8-9871763-6-8 (print)

ISBN # 979-8-9871763-4-4 (digital)

Website: AvaCuvay.com

Facebook Page: AvaCuvayAuthor

❀ Created with Vellum

To everyone in my life who has supported and helped me discover and pursue my own desires.
I hope I have been an equal cheerleader for you in return.

ACKNOWLEDGMENTS

A shout out to my editor, for always being there for me when I push the deadlines I've set for myself but haven't communicated and then send send an email saying "Here's the [very rough first draft that I just finished] story, hope you have time to edit it, and, uh, I kinda need it back in four days or I lose all my pre-orders."

I promise to do better.

CHAPTER ONE

C hrist on a cracker. Ulrik Drekison stood in front of the most beautiful woman he'd ever set eyes on, and two thoughts crossed his mind:

One, he definitely wasn't dressed to impress, having borrowed a mish-mash of clothes from his elderly first-grade teacher Mrs. Olson after working the county fair charity dunk tank.

And, two, he shouldn't care, because the woman in front of him merely represented the competition to his family's logging and construction business.

Plus, rumor had it she was a total bitch.

The severe cut of both her cayenne-red hair and her business suit—an outfit completely inappropriate to wear to a casual county fair, especially in their state of Minnesota where formal attire usually meant the good pair of jeans—bespoke the fact that rumor was likely spot-on.

Still, he probably should have opted against wearing Mrs. Olson's lime green socks with the pizza-slices on them. Or the fuchsia Birkenstock sandals. Or her granddaughter's sweatpants with BABY GIRL printed on the butt. But Mrs. Olson had insisted he change into dry clothes, and Ulrik hadn't wanted to make a scene.

Of course, he hadn't expected to make a business meeting out of the Douglas County Fair opening weekend festivities, either. If he could keep Miss Eydís Helvig, North American Project Manager for Hilda Timbers, in front of him, he just might walk away with a smidge of his masculinity intact.

That was funny. He'd never before had to worry about anyone questioning his masculinity. Being a ripped six-foot-three former high school football star did that. The fact he was a dragon shifter didn't hurt, either. Women flocked to the Drekison brothers, thanks to their Viking good looks and their dragon pheromones. Now that the two younger brothers had fallen in love, Ulrik and Arkyn would get flocked more.

Yet, they both stared, struck dumb, at this particular woman for an awkward amount of time. Arkyn came to his senses first, shaking his head and grasping the hand she offered.

"Oh, for sure, we heard you were coming to town. A pleasure to meet you, Miss Helvig." As the heir-alpha of their clan, and an earth dragon, Arkyn radiated the heady cocktail of CEO swagger and apex predator focus. When he turned the full force of his attention on most women, they blushed and panted, ripe with desire and uncomfortable in their suddenly constricting clothes. This one merely waited with raised eyebrows for him to continue. "I'm Arkyn Drekison of Drekison Logging and Construction."

Miss Helvig shook Arkyn's hand with a firm assurance of her own, her smile bordering on bored. She turned her maple-leaf green eyes to Ulrik.

"*Shake her hand,* fífl." Arkyn sent the mental reprimand to him. The brothers used this handy form of mental communication when at the bars trolling for hook-ups. This was not one of those times, but it snapped Ulrik out of his stupor.

He held his hand out to her. The hand which currently

gripped a cone topped with a giant fluff of blue cotton candy. Her gaze volleyed between the fair food and his face. He switched hands, offering her the empty hand. His left hand. With blue fingers from snacking on the cotton candy.

Sorðinn!

Ulrik's brain rebooted just enough he switched the cotton candy to his left hand, and stuck out his right hand for her to shake. Her small, warm hand slid against his palm with a breathtaking zing of awareness. She gripped his hand—twice the size of hers—confidently enough to make him wonder how she'd fare around his cock. He flinched at the unbidden thought, and his impulsive retreat was no doubt enough for her to assume he was intimidated.

Sorðinn!

Her smile was restrained, yet triumphant. As if she'd won the initial corporate pissing match. Her gaze flicked down his length, which was normally a sign of feminine appreciation. But when her eyes met his again, her expression softened. A little sad, a little sympathetic. Like she thought him to be someone with special needs. Like he had a mental impairment and required her understanding and patience.

He glanced down. The sweats hit him mid-shin and Mrs. Olson's crocheted cardigan stretched and pulled across his muscular chest, his dark blonde chest hair peeking through many of the stitch holes and the yarn flowers distorted beyond recognition. Even his buddy's daughter would know better than to wear this outfit, and she was too young to properly pronounce *froggie,* the word coming out as *fucky* instead, much to her parents' horror.

Streð mik!

"Uh, this is my younger brother, Ulrik." Arkyn made the introduction Ulrik seemed incapable of. Perhaps he did have a mental impairment.

Miss Helvig tilted her head to the side and raised a

challenging eyebrow. Ulrik couldn't bring himself to say it was a pleasure to meet her; that would be a lie. He didn't have the youthful charm of his youngest brother, Ty, the sharp tongue of his brother Ivar, the metal dragon, or Arkyn's confident smoothness. So he cleared his throat and hedged a bit.

"Welcome to Minnesota, Miss Helvig." There, that wasn't so hard, was it? "I hope your presence means Hilda Timbers understands the significance of the Mountain Pine Beetle infestation we're dealing with."

She blinked like she was surprised he could put a complete sentence together. Truthfully, he was rather surprised as well.

"However." Ulrik continued, the conviction in his heart lending his voice a strength and rigidity to rival that of an aak tree. "If they sent you only to figure out where to place the blame rather than how to help fix it, you might as well turn around and go home."

"Slow the roll, dude." Arkyn sent the mental warning, imitating Ty's California girlfriend, Lin. *"This isn't like you."*

True, Ulrik was typically the laid-back one, the peacekeeper between volatile brothers. But this woman—this crisis—had him eager to take up arms and charge into battle.

Miss Helvig crossed her arms, which pushed her full breasts upward, straining against the fabric and buttons of her crisp white shirt. Ulrik tried not to stare. Arkyn tried as well, and the attempt made him look constipated. She shrugged. "And why would you say that?"

It was Ulrik's turn to shrug. "Because it's a problem bigger than any of our individual companies, dontcha know. We need to work together to come up with a solution, or we all lose."

His football days had taught him the importance of teamwork, and that concept had been solidified with the recent invasion by *Niðhöggr*, the prophesized World Destroyer. All the dragon clans had fought together, from his family's Minnesota clan to the New York clan and the homeland Dragon Council of Norway, to defeat the entity.

"Ah. Then it's a good thing I'm here." She purred, stepping closer to Ulrik, not the least bit intimidated by his size, his muscles, or the innate undercurrent of power his dragon exuded. And certainly not the least bit impressed by his good looks. Damn. Looked like she was yet one more woman who preferred his alpha brother to him, the mere second-born son. She side-eyed him, the challenging arch of her manicured eyebrows naturally seductive, as was the throaty timbre of her voice. This was not her first rodeo. Or her first county fair, for that matter. "A pleasure to meet you, gentlemen. I'll see you at the office Monday morning."

She wiggled her fingers in Arkyn's direction, then turned heel and sauntered away, offering both of them an enticing vision of her lush ass.

Before she got lost in the crowd, she threw over her shoulder. "Don't be late, *Baby Girl*."

CHAPTER TWO

W *ell, that could have gone hella better.*
    Eydís berated herself for making such a shitty first impression with the Drekison brothers. Rather than twiddle her thumbs in a second-rate hotel, she'd sought them out as soon as she arrived in town. The first meeting, with the frivolity of the county fair as their backdrop, should have set a professional-yet-not-uptight tone for their working relationship. Instead, she'd managed to spur the second brother into an impassioned speech about responsibility and moral obligation.

Her boss was gonna be so pissed.

She hadn't been sent here to advocate for the greater good. The greater good always cost a company money, and Hilda Timbers preferred to keep its profits to itself. Fortunately, she had the rest of the weekend to mastermind a plan to undo her first impression and reset the dynamics she'd fumbled with the handsome Drekison brothers.

Thoughts focused on this new challenge, she meandered through the crowds at the quaint county fair. Sauntered, like she didn't notice or care about all the shocked stares directed her way. This might be a county fair in the middle of Minnesota, but surely these folks had seen a woman in professional business attire before.

Then again, maybe not. If the stunned reaction she'd received from the two oldest Drekison brothers was any indication, this odd corner of the world might be a little tone-deaf to the impact a power suit could wield. Maybe she needed to rethink her clothing strategy.

She needed attire that was eye-catching in a less deer-in-the-headlights sort of way. While it had been fun to watch two grown men struggle to form complete sentences, especially when she'd crossed her arms to emphasize her cleavage, that was a bad business strategy. Yes, she ran into more than her fair share of men who were stupid, or at least who became stupid when confronted with womanly curves of a Formula 1 road-race level. But men *made* to feel stupid—especially by that same woman— usually responded with anger and combativeness. And she needed the Drekisons to be far less aggressive. She needed them in a position to cooperate and compromise.

Mmmm, Ulrik in a compromising position.

The image of a naked Ulrik fisting his cock flashed in her head and she gasped. Why was she fantasizing about the competition? And why not the sexy, confident oldest brother? Why the second brother, who was either *realllly* comfortable in his masculinity to choose such a horrendous outfit, or had lost a bet. Whichever was true, she shouldn't be fantasizing about him naked, even if it was a huge improvement over his eclectic outfit.

By contrast, it would work in her favor if he fantasized about her. He was a man, and having any of the brothers on the tongue-lolling side of a business exchange could be beneficial. Below-the-belt as it might be, her competitive nature urged her to utilize every weapon at her disposal, and few businessmen were immune to her *womanly charms*. Of course, those businessmen were typically old, unattractive, and married.

The Drekison brothers were anything but.

Her extensive research on Hilda's competition had quickly unearthed the fact all four brothers were young, unmarried, and walking wet dreams. Four stacked and packed Nordic gods toying with the hearts and bodies of Minnesota's unsuspecting female population. Poor gals...they didn't stand a chance. But Eydís could handle the brothers. Not *that* way, because she had no intention of sleeping with any of them. But in a business setting, *she* was the apex predator. She would maul them and their little family business and spit out the bones, with nary a nibble left for the vultures to pick at.

That was her job. One she was singularly equipped to do. Her job title was officially North American Project Manager, but that was merely misdirection. And because Boss Bitch Sent to Destroy Your Livelihood wouldn't fit on her business card.

"Hey beautiful. Come swing a hammer and ring the bell." Some lanky carny called to her from his midway game booth.

Another waved for her to choose his booth. "Toss a ring and win a fish. Three wins gets you a giant stuffed bear."

Eydís didn't acknowledge the offers. She wasn't here for carnival games, a pet fish, or a stuffed bear the size of a Drekison brother. Her job—her life—left no room for any of that. Now that she'd introduced herself, although it could have gone better, she could find her hotel and get some much-needed sleep. Maybe then she wouldn't make rookie mistakes like immediately putting the competition on the defensive. Or assuming the handsome, hulking mass of a second brother had developmental issues just because he was dressed in such a bizarre manner. She hadn't been on her top game, for sure. Instead, she'd put them on edge when she needed them thinking they were all in this together. She needed their guard down. She needed them to welcome her in, not unlike a certain wooden horse of Greek mythology.

Only then could she fulfill her orders. Orders she hated because they came from the same kind of old, unattractive, misogynistic man she spent her days professionally eviscerating. But mostly because her orders would ruin yet another family business and, by extension, another family.

Tearing down another person's family was a special kind of cruel. As someone who lacked any familial ties of her own, she knew all too well how precious they were.

She was *NeiDreki*, an Old Norse term meaning *no dragon*. Deep in her core—her heart, her psyche, her very soul—was an empty space where a dragon should be. She'd been born to a clan of dragon shifters descended from old-world Vikings, yet was bereft of that full heritage because she was empty, having been passed over as a vessel for a dragon.

Such was a fate worse than death for her kind. Embarrassed and scandalized, her parents had sent her away at a young age to live with *humans*, never to be acknowledged by her family or clan again. The dual emptiness that came with missing both a family and a dragon strangled her like the phantom pains of an amputee, her full potential stunted and keening like an injured animal.

She paused in the middle of the fair's frivolity, fists clenched and breaths labored as she fought against the raging turmoil that tried to crush her. Most days, she could ignore the constant pain of her family's abandonment. She could fulfill her employer's expectations and turn a blind eye to the aftermath it wrought on other families. She was merely following orders. Was it the executioner's fault the executed had been deemed unworthy to continue living?

It was a fine line she toed in order to live with herself. And sometimes she stumbled too far to one side. Like now.

At the moment, all her regret threatened to bury her. If she could quit Hilda Timbers and find a nice, comfortable job where this guilt didn't compound, she'd take it in a heartbeat. Unfortunately, only Hilda could withstand her combative nature for any length of time. Withstand and utilize it for their benefit.

Three women stumbled from the nearby beer tent onto the midway path in front of her, distracting her from her internal battle. Two of the women practically carried the third, who seemed more interested in complaining than walking, if the nasally slur of her voice was any indication. "All these years waiting for Ivar Drekison to declare his undying love for me, and the jerk chooses that Norwegian skank who's his cousin. Ew, gross!"

Drekison. For all Eydís knew, Minnesota could be inbred with thousands of people sporting that surname. But she doubted there was more than the one family, and she'd bet her next bonus they were all employed by the company of the same name.

A name that hinted at a similar Nordic dragon-centered culture of her birth heritage. Although that was like assuming everyone with the surname Smith worked with metals.

Drunk girl's friends murmured their condolences with shrugged *could be worse* and *oh, for gross* as the group staggered to the right.

"I don't think she's actually his cousin, Charlotte." One offered with some hesitation. "My mom says the whole family adores her. And ya gotta admit she's really pretty."

"Whose side are you on?" Charlotte glared at her friend as they teetered her back to the middle of the path. "*I'M* pretty, too!"

"I mean, she's pretty in an elegant, European sort of way. She looks like a model."

Nice backtracking. A pretty, model-looking blonde woman who'd caught the eye of a Drekison. These women must be talking about Lucy, who Eydís had met a bit ago when she'd first found the Drekison brothers. That would track, given the vague description Charlotte's friend offered.

"We're on your side, Char." The other one chimed in, tugging up on her friend's jeans as they sagged from the heavy bedazzling on the back pockets. "It's just... well, we've been telling you for years that Ivar isn't all that into you."

This Ivar must be the brown-haired brother holding the huge midway game teddy bear and joked about taking Lucy to the Ferris wheel so they could make out like teenagers. Eydís's job demanded she keep everyone at arms-length, which wasn't difficult because most people annoyed her. But she'd instantly liked both Lucy and Ivar.

Just like she'd been inexorably drawn to the two older brothers, especially Ulrik. Dammit, she needed to stop thinking about him in any manner that wasn't antagonistic.

"Honestly, I don't see why you chose Ivar instead of Ulrik." The first friend said, a slight thread of wistfulness in her voice. "He's way nicer and better looking, if you ask me."

Charlotte blinked at her friend as if considering the suggestion.

Eydís normally avoided drama, but simply couldn't pass up this opportunity to stir the pot a little. It spoke to the chaos currently, constantly, swirling in her soul. "Are you talking about Ulrik Drekison? Of the Drekison Logging Company?" The three girls turned to her, listing a bit from the effort.

"Do you know him?" One asked.

"Yeah, I mean, I just met him." Eydís shrugged, catching Charlotte's gaze, then fanned herself as if the thought of him overheated her senses, which it kind of did if she was going to be honest with herself. "Have you seen his muscles? Gurrrl, *rawr*. He was dressed kinda funny, but he obviously has great *bone structure*, nawmean?"

Truthfully, as ridiculous as the outfit had been, it had cupped and stretched in all the right places, showcasing how large the man was, in all areas. She was woman enough to admit—well, to herself, at least—Ulrik was a walking orgasm.

Too bad she was here to fuck him over in a different, and more unpleasant, sort of way.

Charlotte's face scrunched up. "I never considered the other brothers because I thought... I thought Ivar just needed time." her chin quivered and her voice quavered as if on the cusp of tears. The floodgates opened and she crumpled in her grief, her friends nearly collapsing under the sudden weight, grasping at whatever they could in their frantic attempt to keep upright. Charlotte's shirt hiked to her armpits and she received an accidental wedgie, but it wasn't enough and the threesome tumbled to the ground, Charlotte on the bottom wailing her grief above the cacophony of the midway carnies. "I gaaaave him my virgiiiinityyyyy!"

Eydís clamped a hand over her mouth to avoid laughing too loudly at the drunk girl antics. Blame her exhaustion, but she no longer had the energy to keep her poker face. Especially in the face of such absurd longing for a mere man, no matter how good looking. Even if he was a great lay. There were plenty of fish in the sea, not that Eydís bothered to hook any. Her job kept her too busy. And her naturally abrasive personality ground their dicks down to dust faster than a Dremel power tool.

She snorted in disdain as she skirted the struggling pile of drunk girls and picked her way through the fair to her rental car. She had a job to do. And, in spite of the fact she hated it, she was good at it, it paid her bills, and it provided a legal outlet for her inner anarchy.

She just had to entertain herself until Monday morning so that job could commence.

CHAPTER THREE

> Hey handsome. Wanna meet up for coffee n crullers?

"Why the fuck is Charlotte Larson texting me?" Ulrik muttered to himself as he locked his truck door and walked toward the edge of the woods at their current logging location. Today was Sunday, so everyone else was either at church, at the county fair, or simply spending their day not at work. Like normal people. Which meant he was alone, exactly as he wanted. He had an important task, and witnesses would be detrimental to it.

> Not Ivars phone.

Ulrik shot off the quick response. Why Charlotte had his number was a weird mystery he didn't want to contemplate, as if doing so might conjure the woman herself. A shiver of revulsion ran through him. Their hometown wasn't so large he could guarantee he and his brothers had never fucked the same girl at some point. As the second-born brothers, he'd very likely enjoyed many of Arkyn's sexual cast-offs, and had been the next best thing when Arkyn's hookup for the night had already been selected.

But he'd never knowingly been someone's sloppy second. And the thought of Charlotte redirecting her attention from Ivar to him... he'd watched her on the prowl too many times to wish that on anyone. Least of all himself.

His phoned dinged immediately, but he ignored it, unwilling to address that possible clusterfuck when he already had a crisis to deal with. A Mountain Pine beetle infestation threatened to ruin the family business, in addition to devastating their state's beautiful forests. Since its discovery, he'd spent nearly every waking hour, and countless nightmares, desperate to eradicate this pestilence. But, while he and his Wood Dragon were best equipped to handle it, they couldn't do it alone. The problem required all hands on deck, including the other companies with a vested interest in healthy woods.

These tiny bugs, barely bigger than a fat grain of rice, might not have the prophesized destruction power of *Níðhöggr*, the World Destroyer he and his family had battled less than a year ago, but they were a plague that could destroy the Drekison family's little world. That threat alone was enough for his dragon to crave battle.

And Ulrik allowed it.

Carefully stripping down so he'd have something to wear back into town—he lacked The Hulk's movie magic modesty pants—and putting his phone on silent mode, Ulrik carefully placed his pile of personal belongings atop a wide stump. Then he wandered further into the deep, peaceful silence of the woods.

Punctuated with the distant calls of birds and chitters of squirrels, his barefoot steps were muffled by the mossy, leafy forest floor. Ulrik inhaled deeply, the scent of pine and musty undergrowth energizing his cells like the first light of dawn after a dark and starless night. Sunlight flittered across his face, its heat and intensity softened as it filtered through the dancing canopy of leaves high above. The bit of breeze that escaped brush and eddied around thick trunks lifted the long hair at his shoulders and tickled his throat beneath his beard. Wandering the woods in only the skin he'd been born with heightened his sense of fullness. Wholeness. The sense of rightness, that he was exactly where he was meant to be. It was heady. Sensual. And his dragon quivered to be allowed out to play in his personal Valhalla.

Who was he to deny his beast?

Quickly shifting, his dragon emerged from the deep recesses of his being, like a whale breaching the surface of water from a deep ocean dive. Ulrik let his dragon play for several minutes. The beast cavorted in the woods, winding between the tall trunks and through the branches like the airborne snake it resembled. His dragon's element was the forest itself, and time spent within the silent power of these woods, boasting trees that had lived for over a century, was euphoric. It charged him, powered him. Some magical sort of symbiotic relationship between his dragon and trees revved him more effectively than a Mario Kart power-up or Red Bull energy drink.

The fauna spoke to him. Not in words or telepathically. But he sensed its life, its joy, its pain. Ulrik focused on this pain, letting the sensation lead him to a swath of forest which cried out in withered, debilitated anguish.

This brought him to a copse where the infestation was fresh, the trees already marked with orange paint by the investigation team the combined companies had formed to search out trees in various stages of infestation.

No one could halt the beetles from progressing through the forests like a slow tsunami of destruction, but he and his dragon could strengthen the trees affected if discovered soon enough. Those which had already lost the battle to the beetles would be cut down to remove any lingering threat and make room for new growth. Spraying the untouched trees was an expensive and time-consuming preventive option, but it also threatened to poison the animals in this habitat and contaminate the ground water. The Drekisons had stood soundly against such an invasive solution, and thankfully all the other local companies had sided with them.

Except for Hilda Timbers. That company had been suspiciously silent on the topic, instead sending a representative to *look into the matter further*. Everyone had heard the air quotes in that phrase.

Ulrik shook that thought away, focusing his attention and his dragon's power on the task at hand.

Settling on the ground next to a tree, his dragon pressed its forehead to the trunk below the first spray of branches, the rough bark scritching his scales until he purred in contentment. The purr deepened, softened, searching to match the tree's vibration, the rhythm of its lifeblood. It was there, barely audible but strong. The dragon mirrored the energy, sending waves of it into the tree. Past the protective shield of outer bark, through the softer phloem layer of nutrients, the growing cambium cells where he sensed the hunger of the beetle larvae as they chewed and burrowed, through the sapwood layer acting as the tree's water pipeline, to the pithy center of the heartwood. Now attuned to the tree, the dragon's strength could be shared, lending the tree a predator's nature. The power grew, the vibration expanded until the tree shook with devastating energy unseeable by the human eye. But nature heard it. Birds shot from the upper branches in a flurry of feathers and wingbeats and little critters scampered away. The vibration, contained within the strong, immobile trunk of the tree, worked its way upward and outward until the tree's outer branches and needles clattered against each other as if caught in a blast of wind, raining loosened shrapnel down to earth.

Ulrik sensed the death of the larvae in the wake of the energy blast, and the pine tree began the slow process of oozing the crushed adult beetles through bark holes with sticky sap.

The tree had been saved.

His dragon retreated a step to catch its breath. The forest gave him energy, but this battle technique was unusual. Ulrik and his dragon had always trained for an external battle requiring great physical strength, such as the one against *Níðhöggr*. A fight where their power manifested as weapons of wood and the physical manipulation of trees to defeat an enemy with grand strokes and immense destruction on an Avengers-level scale, leaving an aftermath of devastation to signal the intensity of it all.

Just now, his dragon had defeated an unrelenting army of hundreds, littering the battlefield with their corpses. Yet the area looked no different.

This victory was a silent triumph. A personal war against an enemy he was singularly equipped to battle, where true success would be merely the continuation of their livelihood as they'd come to expect it. He volunteered enough around town to understand how altruistic his part in this war was, even as it felt like a life or death scenario. He would get no recognition for keeping these beloved forests were safe. No feasts of victory. No songs written of his heroic deeds.

And he was okay with that.

Maybe Miss Eydís Helvig, North American Project Manager for Hilda Timbers, would stop looking at him like he was impaired if she knew just how far his commitment to battling this infestation would go. Then again, she could never find out about his shifter half. So it wasn't a question to consider.

He shrugged the thought away and turned back to the task at hand. Now that his dragon had a few minutes to rest, they stepped on to the next tree. This would take hours, they wouldn't save all the trees today, or ever, and he'd stumble home and tumble to bed exhausted, like always. But he'd fight this battle until his last breath.

CHAPTER FOUR

E ydís sat on the uncomfortable stump, scrolling through social media and watching YouTube videos. She'd been here for a couple hours already, having stumbled upon a worksite with a solitary truck parked but no one within earshot to talk to.

Only a pile of clothing and cell phone indicated someone might actually be around the area. Eydís had relocated the pile to a stump closer to the truck and further away from the line of trees. The cell phone, screen locked but lighting up occasionally with increasingly agitated text messages, piqued her attention. She'd never admit it out loud, but she *might* have tilted the phone so she could better see the screen.

She'd listened to too many unsolved murder podcasts over the years to assume waiting for the owner of the clothes and the phone to arrive was a smart move. But she'd been wandering the woods for hours after a harebrained decision to go for a leisurely walk to kill time and clear her head. She was tired. She was sweaty. And the truck had a Drekison & Sons sign on the side. Hopefully she could talk the truck's owner into a quick—and safe—ride back to her hotel. And hopefully that owner would arrive before it got too dark. Her phone battery wouldn't last much longer.

The phone screen atop the sturdy boots lit up again, and she couldn't resist reading it. This one-sided conversation was truly better than any soap opera, and she snorted as the drama continued to unfold.

> Im thru playing nice. Ulrik yur an ass! Y havent u answered ANY of my messages?!

Ooooohhhh. This was Ulrik Drekison's phone? Could this be... maybe... a certain formerly drunk Charlotte on the other end? A Charlotte who had taken a painfully subtle not-subtle or honest hint to pursue him? More importantly if this was Ulrik's phone... were these his clothes?

Eydís clapped at the thought and cackled like an evil villainess.

Her cackle morphed into a groan. Or was that a moan? Who left a pile of perfectly clean and dry clothes at the edge of the woods unless they were going full commando? Or maybe he was taking a swim and had brought another set of dry clothes to change into.

Either way, she might very well get to see him naked. The possibility sent unwanted quivers racing over her breasts, down her spine, to her nether regions. She might be on opposing sides of the corporate conference table, but her body was definitely Team Naked Ulrik.

Eydís thumbed through the clothes. Shirt. Pants. Shoes. Hmmm, no undies or socks. Maybe he wasn't entirely naked. Still, who runs around the forest in just their skivvies?

She might not get to see him completely naked, but he'd be undressed enough to be embarrassed to be seen by her. Which meant he would take her back to her hotel when she asked him. Although, this was the same man who'd walked around the county fair in an outfit that would make a clown blush. Being naked was an improvement on that. So maybe he wouldn't be so embarrassed he could be coerced into driving her anywhere.

Unless the phone and the clothes were there because he'd been abducted and the kidnapper had ordered him at gunpoint to strip down and leave his phone behind. What if she'd sat here for these past two hours while he'd been dragged deep into the woods for some ritualistic sacrifice, or honor killing, or gang-related whack job—

Unnnnghhhh… the image of a naked Ulrik whacking off flashed in her head and she swallowed the sound that was definitely a needy moan.

Why was she like this? Dammit, why did she keep picturing Ulrik naked?

The phone screen flashed again.

> Fine be that way! But youll never get another chance at this booty!

Something was attached—a picture, no doubt—and Eydís urped in her mouth. Had Charlotte sent a picture of her naked butt? Better than her bedazzled option, but, to use her own words from yesterday… *Ew, gross!*

Movement, and the flash of something white, caught Eydís's eye in the growing dusk of the oncoming evening. She looked to the tree line to see—*Holy fucking balls!*—a very naked, and seemingly confused, Ulrik wandering toward the truck, searching the ground and scratching his head like he'd forgotten something important.

Had he forgotten where he'd laid his clothes?

He hadn't yet spotted her, so she looked her fill. Stacked and packed blonde Nordic god was an understatement. He was long and powerful, his muscles rippling yet lacking any unwieldy bulk. His dark blonde hair tumbled past his broad shoulders which sported what looked like twin tattoos, black birds of some sort surrounded by runes. The only ink she could see on his otherwise perfect body. His broad chest had a light dusting of hair that thickened and darkened as it dove straight to his cock, which swayed like an elephant's trunk between his thick thighs.

She'd give up her next bonus if she could get a chance to choke on that dick. She wanted its weight on her tongue, stretch her jaw around its girth, wanted to taste that cream filling. Wanted to fill her palms with the tight muscles of his ass and dig her fingernails into his smooth skin and tickle her nose with his downy navel hair as his cock slid down her throat. Her thighs quivered and slick moisture trickled from her core to her unfortunately serviceable underpants.

If she'd thought to wear her lacy undergarments, the tasty temptation that walked her way might be her next happy meal… and apparently, she'd get to supersize it. Unfortunately, reason flooded her brain as fully as desire had flooded her pussy, bringing her back to baseline and some semblance of self-control. Doubtful that the son of the competition would appreciate a rabid blowjob from a woman who'd pretty much mocked him in front of his older brother at the county fair. And sicced a drunk girl still pining for his younger brother on him. And represented the callous, greedy competition.

"Eydís?" His voice pulled her from her thoughts. He was still thirty feet away, shaking his head as if he didn't believe his eyes. But he made no move to cover himself as he continued to approach. "What are you doing here? With my clothes?"

She flashed him her winningest smile and gave him a saucy little wave. "Heeeeyy. I got a little stir crazy in my hotel room and decided to go for a walk in the forest. Ya know, to kinda see for myself how bad the infestation is. But I got a little lost. Then I got a lot tired. Then I found this truck and figured I'd wait and hitch a ride back."

He didn't call her out for being stupid and walking alone in unfamiliar woods or trusting a stranger. Instead, his face screwed up with an emotion that resembled concern. "You could have called an Uber."

"I. Um." *Damn.* He was right and that would have been the smart thing to do. She stood, shoving her hands in the front pockets of her jeans and shrugging her shoulder in the direction of the truck. "If I did that, I'd miss out on the opportunity to get the company dirt from the truck's owner. Can't very well undermine my competition without it."

Fuuu— Why the hell had she admitted that?! Hopefully it was too dark out for Ulrik to notice the blood rushing from her face. It's one thing to think those thoughts, but to openly admit you were out to ruin their business was a mammoth-sized no-no. Chalk up yet another rookie mistake she was too experienced to make. Her boss was going to flay her. Hell, he probably wouldn't have to bother because, at this rate, she would botch her mission so fantastically that he'd instantly fire her.

Rather than look mortified or aggrieved by her confession, Ulrik simply chuckled and bent down to pluck his pants from the pile. "Could be worse, I suppose."

She blinked at his cavalier attitude about both his nudity and her admitted evil plan as he flicked his pants once, then stepped into them and slid them up his slim hips like this was a locker room and she a teammate. Like he did this all the time. A pang of jealousy lanced her heart for a moment, thinking of all the women he'd been naked around in order to be this blind to modesty.

Speaking of other women...

Ulrik bent to retrieve his phone next, moving with all the unconcerned grace of a mountain lion. Gone were the nerves and the brain-buffering he's exhibited last night. Tonight, he was calm, confident, unruffled.

Men were never that way around her. She made most men nervous, either with her brains, her sharp tongue, or her soft curves. Ulrik's behavior was... comfortable. With her and with his own body. And that was sexier than anything, which did little to keep her thoughts away from wondering how his cock would feel buried to the hilt while she jackhammered him into the mattress.

"Why is she still…" His phone screen flashed bright and he flinched. "Argh!" His phone flew from his hand and he shook it as if burned, his eyes closed and his face scrunched in disgust.

Was the picture of Charlotte's ass truly that gross? "See something you didn't want to?" Eydís hoped she sounded innocently curious.

"You betcha." His voice resigned—no, not resigned… he sounded… exhausted—he pulled his hair back with a sigh and retrieved a tie from his pocket to secure it in a messy man bun. He scanned the ground to find his phone and quickly deposited it with two fingers into his back pocket like it was raw uranium. "Not sure why, but my brother's ex has decided I'm her next conquest."

Not if she wants to live. Eydís's predatory impulse surfaced, instinctively targeting Charlotte as a rival for Ulrik's attentions. She swallowed back the growl that tickled deep in her throat, covering it with a cough. Thank Christ she didn't have a dragon to shift into or that beast would be tear-assing through this clearing to swallow Charlotte whole.

What the actual fuck?

Ulrik had already thrown his shirt on and slid his feet into his boots before she wrangled her nonexistent dragon into submission. He waved toward the truck. "Look, I don't have any cotton candy to offer you today. How about we drive into town, grab some dinner, and I'll tell you all the company dirt you wanna know?"

She crossed her arms, a reflexive action more than anything conscious, and slid him a smile that felt almost genuine. "What, like a date?"

His lips lifted in a half-smile. "Not a date. More like a do-over for last night's poor first impression."

"Sorry, you can't undo a first impression." She smiled and shook her head. Then jerked her chin toward where he'd exited the woods. "Or a second impression."

"Then just dinner between two business associates?"

She pointed a finger at him and narrowed her eyes. "Dinner with a business associate who promised to spill all the tea about his family's company."

"Deal."

He nodded once, then palmed her elbow to usher her to his truck. Eydís recoiled from his possessive move. She didn't tolerate chivalry from men; she was perfectly capable of opening her own doors and shit, and allowing a man to do it for her undermined their ability to see her as an equal. She'd struggled too long and too hard to prove herself in a man's world. There was no way she's allow one little action to undo it and plant her into the weak-and-helpless category.

She yanked on the door handle, realizing too late it was still locked, and looked back at him expectantly. He was going to make her wait, wasn't he? He was going to make her wait until he sauntered over and unlocked his truck, his expression patronizing and looking at her like she was a dumbass for trying to do anything herself.

But he didn't make her wait.

He clicked his fob and she heard the unmistakable sound of unlocking. "Give the running boards a sec to deploy," he cautioned when she flung the door open.

She paused and watched the power-deployed boards swing from under the truck, thankful for the boost they offered. Ulrik's trucks wasn't one of those cringy overcompensating-for-something behemoths—he didn't need one; she'd seen his dick —but she was too short to gracefully climb into his cab without the running board.

He was at her side by that point, and held the door while she hoisted herself in. Was she hearing things, or had he caught his breath when she'd leaned forward as she maneuvered into the truck cab? And why did the thought of Ulrik appreciating her womanly assets please her in a far more personal way than it should?

Their hands brushed as they grabbed for the seat belt at the same time. She huffed, and he stepped back as if understanding she didn't want or need his help. He stepped further back when she grasped the oh-shit bar and leaned out to grip the handle so she could close the door. He didn't comment on her self-sufficiency, or roll his eyes or act as if her actions somehow emasculated him. He merely walked around to the driver's side and climbed in.

Once seated, his gaze traced a path from her suede booties to her face which she felt like a caress from his hands. He started the truck and put the gear in reverse, slanting her a soul-searing smile "Let's get some grub and see if I can make the third impression as memorable as the first two."

CHAPTER FIVE

U lrik was exhausted to the bone. He and his dragon had worked their power on more than fifty trees today, infusing the tree's strength and eradicating the beetles and their destructive larvae. He was both ecstatic and disheartened by the progress. Fifty trees would live and continue to thrive.

Fifty trees out of millions.

There was no way he could save all the trees. Even if he lived to be a hundred, he wouldn't get to all the trees, but the beetles would devastate the forest within a few years. This was a battle he couldn't win, and the truth of it rested like *Mjölnir* on his shoulders and in his heart.

"If you fall asleep on me, *Baby Girl*, I'm eating your burger." Eydís's birdsong voice pulled him from his thoughts.

The same woman who fewer than twenty-four hours ago had walked into his life and set him instantly on edge now sat across the small table from him. And he'd invited her. Yes, she worked for a company renowned for dirty dealing. Yes, she had a business reputation for being aggressive. But she had yet to do or say anything to support any of that.

Plus, keeping your friends close and your enemies closer was a solid strategy. Yeah, that's what he was doing.

In truth, he enjoyed her company, her quick wit, and her teasing smile. He liked her belligerent insistence on doing things herself, such as opening her own car door. He'd been raised to show courtesy, especially to women and the elderly. But he'd also been raised by a strong, capable mother, so Eydís ignoring his help wasn't nearly as unsettling as Charlotte texting him.

He bumped knees with Eydís under the heavily shellacked wooden cocktail round in the corner of his favorite bar, Bunyon's. As petite as she was, she'd had to climb onto the raised stools like she'd climbed into his truck. But the stool and table lacked a support bar above, and she'd nearly tipped. He'd placed a steadying hand on her back, and a zap of awareness had shot down his arm and straight to his cock from the touch. Like when he'd shaken her hand last night.

His dragon had practically purred at the tingling connection, and Ulrik swore he'd find every opportunity to use her height to his advantage if it meant he'd get to touch her. Because, again, he was merely keeping his enemy where he could see her.

But, at the moment, she'd issued fighting words, her lips tugged up on one side in the sauciest smirk, her eyes glinting with delight at the prospect of riling him. He shot her with a challenging glare. "I didn't order a burger. I ordered a Juicy Lucy, dontcha know."

"Same thing. Meat patties and cheese on a bun." She shrugged as she brought her beer bottle to her full lips.

He covered his heart like she'd stabbed it. "Oh, for shame! Allow me to enlighten you, Miss Eydís Helvig, North American Project Manager for Hilda Timbers. A Juicy Lucy is the food of Freyr, the god of virility, prosperity, and plenty. They are grown and harvested in the fields of Gefjon, the goddess of the plow, and bestowed upon we humble Minnesotans because only we are worthy of them."

"God of virility, huh?" Of course she would focus on that.

"A Juicy Lucy is the flawless combination of a thick slice of cheese tucked inside a beef patty to ensure each bite is a melty, savory morsel of perfection."

A melty, savory morsel of perfection. Just like her. And he wanted to take a bite.

The server chose that moment to set their meals on the table, and Eydís looked from his steaming Juicy Lucy to her salad. She couldn't look more disappointed if she were a game show contestant discovering the prize behind door number three was a set of steak knives and not the all-expenses-paid vacation she'd expected.

Ulrik couldn't help teasing her about it. "That bowl of leaves doesn't look quite so appetizing now, does it?"

She issued a jaunty huff and smirked. "I didn't realize my house salad came with a side of bacon." She waved toward the two pieces of thick, crispy bacon poking out from beneath the lettuce like chopsticks.

He snatched one and shoved it in his mouth before she could stop him, her gasp making him smile around the salty, chewy heaven bursting across his taste buds. He'd much rather have his mouth on some of her flavorful parts, but a quick glance at her pretend glare reminded him they weren't lovers. They weren't even friends. And this wasn't a date; it was dinner between two business competitors. As much as he enjoyed their easy comradery, she was not here to play nice.

Stealing her bacon was something business competitors shouldn't do, and he regretted the playful action. He nodded toward his Juicy Lucy. "Would you like half?"

Christ on a cracker. That was also something a business competitor shouldn't do. So why had he? And that whole keep-your-enemies-close crap didn't cut it as an excuse.

She nibbled her bottom lip and stared longingly at his meal, as if she were truly considering his offer. Why did that make his heart beat faster? She looked at him, humor glittering in her eyes. "Am I allowed to? After all, I'm not a humble Minnesotan. I wouldn't want to anger the gods."

Cheeky. He probably shouldn't, but he couldn't help liking her unapologetic spirit, so he raised his eyebrows in challenge. "Didn't take you for someone who worries about offending the gods."

Her expression sobered. "I don't believe any gods are overly interested in people like me." She focused on her salad, spearing a forkful of vegetables like harpooning a fish.

Her words were layered in meaning he didn't fully understand, and they sounded like a midnight confession he shouldn't have overheard. He felt dirty, and not in a fun bedtime frolic kind of way.

Rather than pursue the conversation, he bit into his Juicy Lucy, moaning dramatically around the melty mess to make Eydís further regret her decision to order a salad.

Her tight smile broadened into a genuine grin and she laughed at his antics before stabbing another school of helpless vegetables with her fork. Then she shot him some major side-eye. "You gonna make love to your burger all night so you don't have to answer my questions?"

Ulrik's expression sobered this time. "If I'm making love tonight, it's not gonna be to this Juicy Lucy."

He washed his bite down with the last of his beer and raised his hand for the server to bring them both another. Grabbing several fries, he faced Eydís and nodded for her to begin the interrogation.

Carefully setting down her fork, she inhaled deeply, as if taking the moment to organize her thoughts and focus her questions. "Why were you out in the woods naked today?"

That was the question she was desperate to have answered? He chuckled, liking that she didn't pull her punches. He obviously couldn't give her the full truth. Keeping his family's shifter abilities a secret was second nature. But he could give her a truth. "I know it's weird, but I've always enjoyed walking in nature, *au naturale*. It relaxes me. Energizes me."

She screwed up her face and looked at him askance. "Are you one of those people who fell for the butthole sunning trend?"

He nearly spit out his beer. "Butthole sunning?"

"Yeah, you know, amplify your Vitamin D intake, cleanse your toxins, and align your chakras, or something like that."

"Uh, no. Not a lot of sun in the depths of the forest for any of that." He cleared his throat and shrugged. "When I was young, I imagined the trees could talk to me. But I also thought tying a pillowcase around my neck like a cape gave me the ability to fly, much to my parent's horror when I jumped off the porch and broke my collarbone. These days, I find walking among the trees to be a good way to clear my mind."

"Naked."

"No one's complained about it until today."

"I wasn't complaining." She empaled a bite of salad and met his gaze with her own. She wasn't teasing him.

He tucked that knowledge away for later. You'd think a man who'd enjoyed a steady stream of female appreciation all his adult life would be jaded to the attention, but her words made him smile. She didn't bother to be coy with her sexual attraction. And she hadn't yet sent him a booty pic.

Given his recent experience, that was a bonus.

Before he could respond, she swirled the beer in her near-empty bottle and resumed her questions, lobbing them at him with sniper precision and without mercy. "When was the infestation discovered and by whom?"

"A little over two weeks ago, by my brother Ivar."

"Where did it come from? An infestation doesn't just appear in the middle of a state."

"Don't know. We're working hard to keep it from spreading while the DNR works to track its path and point of origin."

"Why didn't the DNR spot it first?"

"They regulate the state lands, and haven't seen evidence of beetles there yet. And as a government agency, it's possible they're understaffed."

"Have the other companies seen evidence of these beetles?"

"Not to my knowledge, but they understand how crucial it is to contain the invasion lest it spread to their woods."

She canted her head, her eyes narrowing. "Wait, so only your family's woods have been affected?"

"As far as we know, yes."

"How do you know your company hasn't been sabotaged?"

"We don't. Not for certain."

Ulrik leaned closer, crossing his arms on the table in front of him and pinning her with a look. "But why would a local family-owned company risk their own woods and livelihood by sabotaging ours in such a manner? The beetles do not abide by property lines and the preventive treatment is expensive, time-consuming, and results are not guaranteed."

He fisted his Juicy Lucy and chewed slowly, his gaze never leaving Eydís's face. He didn't verbalize the next point, knowing she was smart enough to make that jump of logic. A locally owned company would not sabotage the Drekison's land with an invasive pest. Aside from the fact these family companies had collaborated with one another for generations, another company wouldn't risk their own business with the off-chance they might ruin their competition. But an outside company, a ruthless company large enough with flush holdings in other states to act as a financial buffer against the downturn of one branch, might very well consider sabotage.

What would Hilda Timbers care if nearly the entire state of Minnesota was devastated by a tiny little bug? What would they lose?

What could they gain?

Eydís's face paled, possibly tracking his train of thought and the implications. He put his Juicy Lucy down and dragged several fries through a bog of ketchup as she bristled, tensing as if anticipating an incoming attack. He almost laughed. She didn't know him if she thought he would do that. Full frontal verbal assault was Arkyn's arena. Ulrik was the peacekeeper, the deflector.

Which had always seemed a little out of character for a powerful dragon shifter. His dragon was as fierce and unafraid as the others. He'd trained as tirelessly as his brothers. Had flown into battle against *Niðhöggr* without hesitation and had inflicted as much damage, with the exception of Ty and Lin, who had somehow combined their dragon powers to defeat it. They'd also flown into the entity's guts to do so. They got the bragging rights, and Ulrik was A-OK with that.

Yet in spite of his dragon's honed combat skills, he was most often the voice of reason, offering logic and serenity where the others, Ivar the metal dragon most especially, so often chose action. Maybe because Arkyn and Ulrik were so close in age, and he'd been expected from birth to assume the role of support to the alpha heir-apparent. Maybe the wood element of his beast offered a more balanced attitude: sturdy and unwavering, yet flexible enough to withstand the storm. Whatever the reason that he'd never taken the time or effort to truly dissect, he did not strike while his opponent was distracted. He simply ate his dinner in silence while Eydís worked through her reaction to his unspoken insinuation.

"So, you're accusing Hilda Timbers of planting Mountain Pine beetles in your woods in order to ruin your business?" She squared her shoulders, her voice cold and distant. Gone was the flirty sass. He eyed her fork as she stabbed at her salad again, prepared should she use his hand for target practice.

"I said nothing of the sort." He wiped his mouth with a napkin. "I merely tried to explain why the possibility of sabotage by a neighboring company is unlikely."

"Unlikely. But not impossible."

He shrugged. Her eyes narrowed slightly, anger sparkling in the depths of her green eyes as she continued. "Hilda Timbers might not have had proper representation to assist with this crisis until now. But that does not lessen our commitment to working together to find a solution."

"Interesting." He deadpanned the passive-aggressive Minnesotan phrase, lifting his beer to her as if in salute. "That sounded almost sincere. You must get to practice those words a lot."

Christ on a cracker. That had sounded like something Ivar would say, and he was an unapologetic asshole to most people. Their mother would throttle Ulrik for being so openly antagonistic to a business associate, even if Eydís's true motives were unknown and her reputation didn't instill confidence. He opened his mouth to apologize for his rude words, but her laugh, rich and authentic, stopped him.

Gone was the flashing anger and tension. Her smile spread across her cherubic face and she lifted her own beer to salute him. "Yes, I have had plenty of practice with those words. You have no idea."

She impaled him with her shrewd gaze as easily as she had her salad. "And you promised to answer all my questions about your company. I've barely begun."

Humans would never connect his family's logging and construction business with mythological creatures such as dragons. And since that was be the only topic he could not discuss with a human, Ulrik did not hesitate to confirm his promise. He nodded to the server for another round of beer, then spread his arms wide as if he had nothing to hide.

"You are correct, I agreed to that." He smiled to match hers, oddly invigorated by the prospect of spending more time with her. "Ask away."

CHAPTER SIX

E ydís rubbed her temples, willing the coffee to hyperspeed into her veins and dispel the hangover pounding her head with all the throbbing intensity she'd wanted Ulrik to pound her body with last night.

But he hadn't pounded her. Because they were corporate adversaries, he was a gentleman, and she'd gotten drunk.

She'd matched him beer-for-beer, which was nothing to brag about since she was half his size and about a third his muscle mass. Somewhere between beer number five and beer number... something in the double digits... she'd wanted to fuck him more than she wanted self-respect, and who could blame her? Fortunately for her morning-after regrets, they hadn't fucked. From what she could tell, they hadn't even kissed, although that part of the night was a tad blurry. She couldn't remember the details between the bar and waking up alone and in her clothes this morning, which was a stupid position for a single woman in the company of a practical stranger to put herself in.

On the positive side, she also couldn't remember a time she'd had so much fun.

She'd initially tried her damndest to extract valuable

information about the Drekison business. As promised, Ulrik had been an open book. He'd answered all her questions without hesitation and with an honesty that couldn't possibly be genuine. The Q & A session had somehow veered wildly off-course, and she'd also learned that the Drekisons were about as Midwest down-home wholesome as a family could possibly get—the man mowed his elderly first grade teacher's lawn every week, for cryin' out loud—and she wanted to get to know them all better.

And she shouldn't want that! Not if she was going to succeed with her mission.

Even their imperfections were perfect. Like how his mom was in a heated war with another woman over who brought the tastiest hot dish to the church pitch-ins. Or how Arkyn had once made a game-winning touchdown after a uniform malfunction caused his pants to slip down, so he'd run seventy yards while everyone else in the stadium gaped at the 100% GRADE A BEEF "tattoo" some girl had Sharpie'd on his butt cheek the night before.

Her stomach muscles still hurt from laughing so much. Her face hurt from smiling. And now, her head hurt from alcohol consumption. Proper punishment for having enjoyed what the world would view as a date with the son of her competition.

Dragging a long, hot sip from her venti and wishing she had three more, Eydís pulled her rental car into a parking spot at the Drekison & Sons office, a simple log cabin perched like a postcard at the edge of their family's woods. This Monday morning meeting was the Come to Jesus with all the local logging companies to discuss the beetle infestation. She inhaled deeply, then exhaled slowly. Oddly enough, facing Ulrik this morning after their non-date date might be the balm she needed for what was surely going to be a tense morning filled with angry posturing and finger-pointing. A girl could hope, at least.

"Good morning, Miss Helvig." Arkyn's deep rumble pulled her attention from her brooding, and she faced the oldest

Drekison brother as he strolled up the sidewalk. He was exceedingly handsome with his sky-blue eyes, blonde hair curling in gentle waves past his shoulders, the top half pulled away from his stunning face, and darker blonde beard lending him a sexy lumberjack look to complement his Friday corporate-casual outfit that made love to his muscular physique.

He was a walking wet dream. So why didn't the view send shivers of arousal down to moisten her panties, like thoughts of—

"A pleasure to see you again, Eydís." Ulrik's morning-rough voice nearly tugged a moan from her. She clenched her thighs against the instant bloom of arousal as he stepped from where he'd trailed his brother. He wore his hair down with a careless windblown grace, jeans, boots, and a basic waffle weave Henley shirt in an aqua blue that made his ocean eyes pop and her mouth water. Not as much as seeing him naked, but yeah, she was suddenly very thirsty.

Before she could do anything more embarrassing than choke on a gulp of too-hot coffee, he lifted the enormous pink box he balanced in one hand. "Care for a donut? Emerson's Bakery makes crullers that melt in your mouth."

His lips lifted in a smile that was oblivious to the fluttering effect his words had on her nerves. She desperately wanted him to offer her something for her mouth. Or maybe she'd melt in his. Either way, his innocent offer gutted her, mostly because he appeared completely unaffected by the evening they'd shared.

And she bristled at the result.

"Trying to sweeten me up, Ulrik?" She crossed her arms and hiked a skeptical eyebrow.

He flashed a 100-watt smile. "I wouldn't dream of it, *lítill fura*. Your prickly spirit would not melt as easily on the tongue as sugar." His voice dipped to a growly purr she felt to her core like her battery-powered BFF. "But to have your glaze coat my mouth would make the effort worthwhile."

Dammit, the sensual image of his tongue on her assaulted her frail attempt to remain unaffected, and she ground her teeth. While she'd gleaned no helpful information from him last night, he'd apparently figured out he could manipulate her with his utter sexiness. That wouldn't do. *She* was the one who led men by their needy dicks. Not the other way around.

Before she could say anything, Ulrik continued as if he hadn't just made her panties moist. "We are looking forward to your insight today. It might be exactly what we need to find a solution to our problem."

Wait, what? They *wanted* her opinion?

Arkyn beat her to the door handle and opened it for her, much to her chagrin. She could open her own doors, thank you very much. He cleared his throat. "I'd like to add a point of clarification."

Here it came. The good cop to Ulrik's bad cop. Or maybe it was the other way around.

Arkyn leaned his head close and lowered his voice, a sly glance toward his brother. "That Grade A Beef tattoo? Ulrik dared the girl to do it while I was passed out drunk. And then he cut the elastic on my football pants." Arkyn leaned closer and winked. "You must keep your eyes on him."

Ulrik chuckled. "It was merely retribution. The week before, you stole my clothes from the locker room. I had to run three blocks naked to catch up to the bus."

"*Fifl*, the first ten years of your life you spent naked more often than not." Arkyn snorted.

"Not much has changed." Eydís muttered under her breath as Ulrik snorted. Great, now she pictured him naked again.

"Only because I had to wear your hand-me-downs." Ulrik glared at his brother, but there was no true heat in his gaze or his words. Was this simply what siblings did? She wouldn't know. But, given the stories he'd had shared last night, it would track.

She looked at him and raised an eyebrow. "Were you wearing his hand-me-downs yesterday?"

He merely shrugged, unapologetic, while Arkyn threw his head back in laughter.

"Boys, we're not paying to air condition the outdoors." An older male voice came from inside the office.

Arkyn and Ulrik straightened, but looked entirely unrepentant as they waved for Eydís to step first into the surprisingly spacious cabin. A couple dozen men, most middle aged and dressed in jeans and flannel shirts, stood in the open-concept area, mingling and drinking coffee.

And judging her.

She'd been in this spotlight hundreds of times. As a woman in a predominantly male industry, she was used being sized up and found lacking, stared at as if she'd grown scales and wings. Pandering, mansplaining, coddling, unwanted sexual advances, and outright hostility. She was her company's first responder, and these meetings were the burning buildings she was expected to run into and save.

Well, not *save* so much as allow to strategically burn until the owners were willing to salvage what little they could and sell at a pittance to Hilda Timbers.

This was her battlefield, and her blood sang at the carnage she could wreak. The destruction somehow soothed the nonexistent beast deep inside her for a moment. Gave temporary purpose to that emptiness.

One man stood center of the cabin, tall and fit with broad shoulders and a remarkable resemblance to the two brothers who flanked her. Bright blue eyes, full lips, and an immaculate salt and pepper mane of hair pulled away from his face with side braids ending in silver beads, his full beard much the same: manicured and sporting two braids. From her research, this must be the father. For a middle-aged man, he was hot as hell.

No wonder Ulrik and Arkyn were so panty-melting. It was in their DNA. How did the women of Minnesota survive?

Another man stepped to the father's side. He was a slightly younger version with a more emo-barista appearance due to the stark sideswept undercut and the shorter beard. Both men faced Eydís, their smiles warm and welcoming.

Not the greeting she normally received in these meetings.

"You must be the representative from Hilda Timbers." The older man's words held a slight foreign accent, likely a combination of the Norwegian heritage Ulrik had told her about and his years in Minnesota. "I'm Jólnir Drekison. This is my brother, Bodil. You've already met two of my sons. Welcome to our little corner of Valhalla."

Valhalla? The Drekisons sure liked their Viking mythology references. Ulrik had waxed poetic about his burger last night, invoking Viking gods. His shoulder tattoos hosted Nordic runes, same as Jólnir's hair beads. Add to that the fact they all looked like Viking warriors who'd traveled in time and were forced to wear modern clothes. All evidence pointed to a not-so-distant Northern Europe heritage, much like that of her own New York clan. Well, *former* clan, where she'd spent the first five years of her life before being tossed away because she didn't host a dragon. Because she was considered useless without one. Because her parents couldn't find it in their heart to love her in spite of being *NeiDreki*.

Anger bubbled up, hot and destructive, at the reminder she hadn't been good enough for her own family to keep her. Only her employer acknowledged her skills and put up with her combative nature.

The reminder grated on her more than a face against moving pavement.

She grasped the father's offered hand, his grip warm and comfortable. Unlike every other meeting she'd endured, this was not a pissing match between competitors. At least, it wasn't *yet*.

That simple fact made her smile, and it felt mildly authentic in spite of the angst swirling in her soul. "Hello, Jólnir. Bodil. I'm Eydís Helvig. It's pleasure to meet you."

Introductions continued around the room. From her studies on the neighboring companies, these men were exactly who she'd anticipated, all of them heavy hitters in this industry and neck of the woods. Big fish in a small pond, especially compared to Hilda Timbers which had interests in multiple states. But that fact did not lessen the importance these men represented or the swagger they had every right to claim. Yet, even in a room of self-appointed business leaders, her attention continued to gravitate to the Drekison men like a compass pointing true north. She was keenly aware of them, particularly Ulrik, a fact which both soothed and agitated.

All of them, from father to uncle to sons, exuded power and a big-dick energy none of the others in the room could match. And those who tried looked pitiful by comparison. Whatever else any of the other men said or did, the Drekisons ruled the room with their quiet authority.

Once introductions were made and everyone grabbed a donut, they congregated around the war-room-style table. Larger than her king-size bed, it held detailed maps of the Minnesota forests, park and company property lines marked, as well as a clear overlay that tracked areas where the beetle infestation had been noted, cleared, or as-yet uncharted.

The pattern was alarming. At least for the Drekisons. Their properties were swathed in red, indicating large areas of infestation. Within those areas, Jólnir marked sections of trees that had already been cleared, the dead, dried wood sent to the sawmills for processing when possible. Otherwise, they were cut into logs and burned onsite.

"We've roasted a lot of marshmallows these past few weeks." Bodil admitted with a chuckle and a pat to his flat belly.

The others laughed. But Eydís was too busy pondering the

information on the map. Something didn't add up. The beetles were found primarily on Drekison lands. If the invasion was like other pests, traveling in a giant swath from one region of the country to another, like an enormous football stadium fan-wave, then all the companies should all be suffering the effects of the pests. The map showed only the tiniest spots of infestation on the lands of the other companies.

There was no proof, but she sensed in her gut this infestation wasn't random. Something was rotten in the state of Minnesota.

As the others chatted and joked and drank their coffee, Eydís spoke softly to Ulrik, sweeping her hand to indicate the maps on the table. "What are the sources for all this information?"

"All the red showing beetle sightings? Several companies sent guys to help us canvas Drekison lands."

"What about the others? Didn't you reciprocate?"

"They didn't ask for our help." He shrugged.

"So, no outside source has confirmed the accuracy of their reports?"

He shook his head.

With no accountability, the other companies could report whatever they wanted. She pondered the various strategies. If the other companies under-reported their own infestations, what benefit would they gain? What if they had over-reported them?

Sonuva—

"And how do the beetles spread?" She raised her voice, cutting through the casual chatter. All eyes swiveled to her as she addressed the DNR officer. He was about her age and related distantly to one or more of the other families so they'd asked him to join the meeting. If she'd offered to give him a hand job, he couldn't have looked more excited, grabbing his belt and hefting it over the paunch he already sported.

"Well, there are a few ways they spread." He channeled his inner John Wayne. If he called her *Little Missy* or *Darlin'*, she'd have to throw hands. "The two most common are for the grown beetles to take wing and fly, or for infected wood to be introduced into a new area. Ya see, that means—"

"Thank you for the explanation, Owen." Ulrik interrupted with a soft, but firm voice, his expression every bit a predator ready to pounce. "I believe Miss Helvig asked that question simply to make a point."

Did her jaw drop open? She'd never had a man back her up like that. Hell, she'd never had anyone back her up. She'd always had to fight her battles alone.

Owen looked at her as if to verify Ulrik's statement. She smiled and nodded. "He's not wrong. The Drekison woods are bordered by parks with camp sites. If the beetles arrived from infested campfire wood, that would certainly reflect poorly on park personnel and policies."

"B-but we have signs posted telling people to buy where they burn. That firewood not sourced locally can spread pests." Owen blathered as if already backed into a corner.

"There are speed limit signs posted along all the state roads. Can anyone in this room claim they've never pressed their luck to go faster?" She looked around the room, but no one nodded or raised their hand. She speared Owen with a pointed look. "And those speed limit signs are law, not suggestions."

Owen fidgeted under the weight of her stare, his mouth opening and closing and his eyes popping wide like a county fair carnival goldfish. "Well, the DNR is understaffed. We can't check everybody." He offered up the lame excuse. Ulrik had said the same thing last night. She merely cocked her head, waiting for a better excuse.

Someone cleared their throat and spoke. "There are state woods and parks all over Minnesota, Miss Helvig. It would be a logistical nightmare to expect the DNR to police every person using them."

"Parks might be open to the public, but they do not have open borders, Mr. Clausen. They have defined entrances staffed by the DNR." She slanted the man a withering smile, then directed her next words at Owen. "If everyone's lands were suffering from a beetle infestation, DNR staffing issues or natural beetle flight patterns could possibly be blamed. But these maps indicate the issue to be far less random than those excuses would have us believe."

No one spoke, stunned into silence by her words, staring at her as if unsure how to respond. Anger—at having their bullshit called out?—simmered beneath that shock. This was a stand-off the likes of the O.K. Corral. Whether she was Wyatt Earp or Ike Clanton remained to be seen.

Pffft. Call her Clanton because there was no chance she was the good guy in any of this.

CHAPTER SEVEN

The entire room stared at Eydís as if she'd grown two heads. With a pleasant smile on her lovely face, she'd accused the DNR of gross negligence. And then hinted at a pointed attack on Drekison lands.

In truth, the whole Drekison family had already arrived at that same conclusion, but couldn't say anything. It was one thing to accuse one's neighbors of such without undisputable evidence. But for an outsider to connect the dots so quickly, and so vocally, was far more impactful. Eydís had shocked all the other CEOs into a stupefied silence.

Ulrik bit his tongue to keep from laughing.

"*She has the heart of a true shield maiden.*" Father spoke through the mental connection the Drekisons shared, admiration apparent in his voice. "*I'm glad she's on our side.*"

"*We shouldn't assume she's on any side but her own, Father.*" Ulrik countered. He might struggle to keep his attention on the meeting and not on the way her navy power suit hugged her lush ass and pushed her full breasts together beneath the silky turquoise blouse, but he had no doubt she played this game solely for her own benefit.

"Even the Allfather does not stand alone. She may yet decide we are worthier as allies than as opponents. Give her time."

Eydís glanced at them, her brows furrowed in confusion as if she'd heard their conversation and wondered why they spoke of her in such a manner. Ulrik smiled and nodded, even though she did not need his encouragement. She blinked and shook her head as if to dispel her confusion.

"She's feisty. I like her. We should invite her to dinner." Bodil's lighthearted words made Ulrik smile.

"Get in line, Uncle. Ulrik likes her as well." Arkyn's teasing remark made Ulrik scowl.

Eydís glanced at them again. Specifically, at Ulrik, blinking in shock.

"Miss Helvig, surely you can't believe a few pieces of bad firewood snuck into a public park can cause such a sudden and wide infestation." Larry Olson interjected, his voice just this side of patronizing. One glance at Eydís proved she was every bit the shield maiden Father had claimed: She smiled like this was Sunday brunch even as fury rolled off her so thick Ulrik's bones ached with it. If Father ever spoke to their mother in such a tone, she'd grind him up and serve him in her next church potluck hot dish. Ulrik's dragon ached to snap a bite of the lanky son of Uncle Bodil's friend. But Eydís could defend herself. And for him to step in as if she was weak would be as belittling as Larry's words and tone.

Shield maidens fought alongside. Not behind.

When Eydís spoke, her voice dripped with saccharine sweetness. "No, Larry, I don't believe that. Only an idiot would jump to that conclusion."

Larry blinked as if she'd smacked him, then scowled at her audacity. Ulrik had called him an idiot to his face at least a dozen times over the years, and the man had laughed it off. All the men in this room had been brutally honest with one another for decades with no hard feelings. Yet an outsider comes in and does the same, and suddenly they're offended, judging by the expressions around the room. Or was it because she was a woman? If they wore pearls, they'd be clutching them.

Ulrik bit his tongue again. This must be how Eydís had earned her reputation as a total bitch: calling businessmen out on their idiocy.

Before anyone could respond, she addressed the room. "Gentlemen, I'm not here to point fingers. I'm only here as an equal with the same vested interest in thwarting this infestation as all of you—"

"No offense, Miss Helvig, but you aren't an equal." David Peterson interjected. He was the eldest of the group, attending with his son and grandsons. All the Peterson men were hardworking pillars of the community, but David leaned toward too much good-ol'-boy for Ulrik's taste. The older man nodded to indicate everyone in the room. "We are all independent businessmen who own our companies and make the crucial decisions needed to keep them solvent. We live and die by the decisions we make. You are a merely a Hilda Timbers employee."

"No offense taken, Mr. Peterson, because your opinion of me doesn't matter." Eydís stood straight and still, like a lioness before the attack, her voice firm and unyielding. "I may not own Hilda Timbers, but if I fail in my duties or if, by my own negligence, I cause the company significant losses, I will lose my job. So, I live and die by what we decide here today as much as any of you."

"You can always get another job." David countered.

"You can always start another company."

"Oh fer cryin' out loud!" David had never lost his cool so quickly before. "Ya can't just come in here and tell us how to run our businesses!"

"All who come to this table carry an equal right to be heard, David." Father's calm voice swept away the aggression roiling in the room before David could rile the room further. "Hilda Timbers sent Miss Helvig as their representative, so she deserves our respect accordingly. You are welcome to leave if your company's best interests are no longer being met."

Father was a water dragon, his power as deep and insuperable as the currents of the ocean fathoms below the dancing surface. Now, like so many times Ulrik could remember, Father's calm dominance redirected the turbulent waters of a meeting to a calm forward flow until everyone's focus aligned like boats sailing as a unified armada. He'd earned such a reputation for it, he rarely had to pull on his dragon's power of influence anymore.

But he did now. Ulrik sensed his father's dragon prowl, and Ulrik's own dragon stretched and danced in anticipation of a skirmish. Gritting his teeth and promising the insistent beast some playtime later, he tamped the dragon down before its green scales could surface along his bare arms. A room full of humans would not take kindly to that sight.

Eydís whipped her attention to Father, shock and confusion widening her emerald eyes. Her gaze volleyed between the four Drekison men as if searching for something she couldn't name. Had she sensed the undercurrent of power? Had she somehow sensed their dragons? That would be...unusual. And troublesome. Most humans would never understand what it meant to be dragon shifters, a fact which he and his brothers were ever-mindful of when dating. Ty and Ivar were lucky enough to have found dragon shifters to love. Unless Ulrik traveled to the New York clan or to—ugh, no thank you—the Norwegian Dragon Council, he was destined to marry a human woman. He just had to find one who would not be freaked out by his dragon.

Uncle Bodil had been that lucky. Aunt Steph was fully human, as were their children, having been born *NeiDreki*. Even being human, she was as fierce as Ulrik's mother, so marrying and mating with a shifter had never worried Aunt Steph.

She was a spirited shield maiden for Uncle Bodil.

Would Ulrik find such a woman for himself? Could Eydís be that woman?

David Peterson grumbled at Father's words, but stood down from his face-off with Eydís. All eyes looked to Father to say something. This was typical when his dragon's powers drifted through the room, the humans instinctively submitting to the beast's superior strength which Father wielded with expert dexterity.

Normally, he would steer a meeting back to the topic at hand. Instead, he looked at Eydís, and dipped his chin in the barest of nods. Ulrik smiled. With that simple and subtle motion, Father conceded to her the authority to direct the meeting and those in attendance.

She blinked, stupefied. Had no one ever given her such power so readily? An unfortunate miss because Eydís was clearly born to lead. With a deep inhale, she once again addressed the room. "Gentlemen, I am here to work with all of you on a strategy to defeat the beetle infestation. Can we at least agree that any successful battle strategy must first take stock of strengths and weaknesses?"

When the men around the table nodded or grunted their agreement—some more readily than others—Eydís's lips curved in a smile so genuine and triumphant, Ulrik nearly cheered. He had no experience or understanding of the gauntlet a strong woman like her must brave in a testosterone-filled meeting such as this, but this mutual, if begrudging, acquiescence from the room felt like a victory for her.

She continued. "Your willingness to be here today is a strength. Your strength of community and commitment to stand by one another in the face of a common enemy, like brothers-in-arms."

Ulrik noticed she did not include herself in that statement.

She captured everyone's attention, her triumph bleeding into tension. Ulrik suspected what she was about to say would tilt their world on its axis. She drew in a deep breath and squared her shoulders. "Unfortunately, someone—very likely someone in this room—is sabotaging the Drekison's lands."

The room erupted. Men yelled at her and waved their hands in all directions as if this was some poorly choreographed flash mob. They scowled and shook their fists and murmured in disdain, yet she stood still, shoulders back and chin lifted. This was definitely not her first rodeo. Or her first solo battle.

That fact didn't comfort Ulrik.

Only the Drekison men remained calm and focused in light of this bombshell. Because it wasn't such a bombshell for them. The outrage permeating the room grew in volume and intensity, until Father held up a hand. The room quieted, but the vibrations of offense and anger did not diminish.

He looked directly at Eydís and spoke with calm authority. "Miss Helvig, please explain what brought you to this conclusion."

With a nod, she enumerated them. "No surrounding states or Canada have reported any significant evidence of beetle infestation. Neither are there any notable infestations elsewhere in Minnesota with the exception of Drekison lands. And it would appear the epicenter of the infestation is in the middle of your woods."

She looked at each man in the room, her eyebrows lifted in challenge, her voice soft but firm in the stunned silence. "Infestations don't simply appear, gentlemen. Someone, with purposeful and malicious intent, trespassed onto Drekison land and planted enough beetles to destroy their business."

Ulrik expected another uproar. Instead, there was silence. Whether shocked by the implications of her accusations or guilty of them, he couldn't determine. All eyes remained on Eydís and the tension at the corners of her lips and eyes proved she did not like being the bearer of such bad news.

Larry Olson cleared his throat. "Just because you're the one to make the accusation doesn't mean Hilda Timbers can't be the guilty party."

Arkyn jumped on that with a snort. "Dude, we're not twelve. This isn't a *he who smelt it, dealt it* situation, dontcha know. If we've been the target of such an attack, everyone is a suspect."

"True. My own company as much as any." Eydís agreed, her stance rigid and her hands fisted at her side. Her tension was a physical entity and Ulrik wanted to wrap her in his arms and assure her all would be okay. His dragon whined at the need to comfort her, not that she would welcome it from anyone, especially not at the moment when still trying to prove herself to these men. And maybe not even afterward in private.

She swallowed hard and faced Father for the first time since he'd given her the figurative gavel. "Mr. Drekison, it would be unwise to assume anyone is innocent, including your competitors and your own employees."

Father smiled at her, unbothered by her revelation and the apparent sabotage of their lands. Because it wasn't news to the Drekisons. He bowed his head to acknowledge the part Eydís had unwittingly played in the hand their family had played. "I agree, Miss Helvig. Thank you for your thoughtful insight."

CHAPTER EIGHT

She was going to lose her job.

"Frank, it couldn't be a clearer case of sabotage if the beetles spelled out the word with all the trees they've killed." She gripped the steering wheel of her car while her boss reamed her a new one over her cell phone's speaker.

"Eydís, I don't care *why* the forests are dying." Frank Hilda, VP of Operations, was every bit like the businessmen at this morning's meeting, only more so, with a larger sense of self-importance and a shorter tolerance for incompetence. His tone made it clear her performance fell on the wrong side of his expectations. "I only care about the fact an infestation gives us prime opportunity to buy out all the owners. *And* the fact you accused your own employer of said sabotage."

The last bit was growled, his anger vibrating over the cellular data like a living beast. She'd witnessed his ire before, and had often been the recipient of it. He was a focused businessman with high performance expectations of his staff. So she shouldn't feel so blind-sided by his comment. But the report she'd submitted immediately following the meeting had been very top-level and sparse on interpersonal details; how could he know she'd lumped Hilda in with all the other possible saboteurs?

She wanted to ask, but her immediate concern was deflecting his anger. "I did not accuse Hilda Timbers of sabotage. I merely agreed that anyone could be a suspect."

A minor, if important, difference, especially when her job was on the line.

"Dammit, we're trying to buy the bastards out!" The growl mutated into a roar. "Not march down Main Street in lockstep with them!"

Eydís clenched her teeth against the volume that rang tinny and screechy in her car, grateful no one else could hear him. No need for the world to know she'd royally fucked up.

But she knew. Her hands shook. Hopefully her voice did not. "It was a move to gain their trust, Frank. This is a chess match, as you well know. I can't go straight to checkmate. It requires finesse, and sometimes that means sacrificing a pawn. Today, that pawn was to lump Hilda with the others."

Hopefully Frank bought that excuse, though that hadn't been her actual intent at the time. For once in her career, she'd spoken straight from the heart without first filtering it through her job parameters. She knew better; she just hadn't anticipated it would come back to bite her so soon.

"You are correct, Eydís. Sometimes a pawn must be sacrificed." His easy agreement set off an alarm bell in her head, but she dismissed it. She'd been worried about her job since the meeting, and this call simply confirmed the fact she needed to do better.

"Frank, more important here is the fact only one company has an infestation. The original plan depended on *all* the logging company lands being at risk. No one is going to panic and sell to us."

"They will when the infestation gets bad enough. You just have to make that happen."

Eydís inhaled to calm herself, thankful the country roads were barren of other drivers. She didn't need the double challenge of safe driving while also navigating the minefield that was her boss. "Please clarify your expectations. Short of me somehow trapping millions of Pine Mountain beetles myself and trespassing onto the lands of the other companies to release said beetles, there will be no further infestation. And even then, it could take years to get to a critical level, which it won't, because all the companies are now aware of the threat."

"All we need is one domino to topple. It will take the rest of them with it."

His cryptic words only confused her. Did he think the Drekisons would lead the panic, giving up and selling to Hilda? She shook her head, not that Frank could see it. "Don't count on the Drekisons to be that domino. In light of the extent of damage and the threat of sabotage they've experienced, they aren't a bit shaken or worried."

"Yes, I'm aware you seem to have insider knowledge of that family." The accusation was clear in his voice, like she'd somehow betrayed him by doing her job. "I will expect you to use that to our advantage."

Her heart raced. She didn't want to ask, but had to hear it for herself. "And how do you suggest I do that?"

"You're too smart to make me spell this out." The deep chuckle on the other end was dark and humorless. "You're a woman. Keep them distracted until I get what I want."

That didn't sound ominous or anything.

"Frank, I may be a woman, but I'm not a whore!" But he'd had already hung up. Eydís couldn't breathe. She'd done some underhanded shit for her employer in the past. But she'd never done anything illegal. And he'd never asked her to so thoroughly mix her personal and private life. Or that of their competitors.

The good news was that she hadn't been fired. Yet.

Eydís pulled the car over and rested her head against the

steering wheel, her heart racing, her chest heaving, and her gut simultaneously rolling and clenching so violently, she might vomit.

This wasn't how her trip to Minnesota was supposed to go. She was supposed to breeze in, make a half-assed show of working with the others to find a solution, drop the subtle hints the infestation was insurmountable and perhaps they should sell before they lost their shirts. Instead, she found only one company with any significant infestation, owners who seemed oddly unconcerned about that fact, and evidence someone was trying to destroy them.

And she couldn't be certain her own company wasn't to blame.

Eydís sat back and closed her eyes, forcing deep, steady breaths, counting to ten until her heart calmed and her hands stopped shaking. She counted to ten again because the first time hadn't worked.

She continued for several counts of ten.

This wasn't her. She wasn't one to get so emotionally overwhelmed, especially where a job assignment was concerned. She was always calm and collected and in charge. She was the alpha, the predator, the—

"Who the fuck am I kidding?" She grumbled to the idling car. "I wasn't any of that today."

She'd love to blame that on the four handsome Drekison men who had welcomed her, supported her, openly backed her in front of long-time peers, and been utterly so... so... so damned *nice*. She'd love to blame them, but it wasn't their fault she had been uncharacteristically off her game. And to be honest, if she had it to do again, she would change nothing.

The Drekisons called to something deep inside her.

Something in a hidden corner of her soul reached for them. An invisible tether connected her to them, like their fates were somehow intertwined. Or perhaps it was as simple as the fact that the Drekison men seemed undaunted by the possibility they might lose everything. Had, in fact, thanked her for bringing this devastating news to light.

And then invited her to join the family for dinner.

Who even did that? And why was she second-guessing her decision to grab a case of beer instead of a nice bottle of wine so she didn't arrive empty-handed? Why was she excited to spend an evening with their family?

Squaring her shoulders and shaking off the unease left by her conversation with her boss, Eydís put her car in drive and pulled back onto the road, continuing for another mile or so before her map app instructed her to turn into a driveway hidden by the thick tree line following the road.

The driveway was a long, winding gravel tunnel through a sweeping arbor of lush tree branches overhead, their leaves beginning the glorious journey toward shades of orange and yellow. Sunlight through the leaves dappled her car's hood like she traveled some magical portal to a fey kingdom. The road ahead curved to the left and the passageway opened up, no doubt to an enchanted clearing where the lovely Drekison homestead would stand, dripping in ivy vines and surrounded by a moat of wildflowers. Eydís half-expected *Lord of the Rings* adventure-music to play as she followed the driveway toward where Ulrik and his brothers had been grown to be the confident, powerful men they were.

She blinked as a 1970s split-level home with a two-car garage came into view. The house sported several garden gnomes in the strip of bushes and flowers along the front, a basketball goal rusty from disuse, a large shed further in the back, and what looked to be a combination fire-pit-slash-wood-chopping ring nearest the trees.

Eydís stared at the house, mouth open and laughter bubbling up her throat. She shook her head at her stupid fanciful imaginings and parked next to the first of several trucks resting along the side yard. "Oh, gurl. This isn't a fantasy movie. They're normal people like me."

Not true. The Drekisons were a nuclear family with parents who'd stayed married and grown children who still talked to them. By contrast, Eydís had grown up in the foster care system, fighting for the few resources available, hopping from one family to the next so often she'd barely made a dent in her pillow before being relocated. She was too headstrong, too combative, too... feral... for anything to last.

Not much had changed. She was still combative and headstrong. And possibly feral. Just in nicer clothing and with enough manners to not arrive empty-handed.

Tossing aside her ugly childhood memories, Eydís focused instead on dinner with the nice, wholesome Drekisons. Maybe an evening spent with them would help temper her prickly personality and give her inspiration for how to make her boss happy without having to resort to fucking them over.

A girl could hope.

She plucked the case of beer from the passenger seat and headed toward the house. She'd passed her own bumper as a red truck pulled onto the lawn next to her. A man who looked like a brunette version of Ulrik and Arkyn hopped out and waved to her as he rounded the truck to the passenger side. "You're that Eydís gal from Hilda Timbers. We met at the county fair."

A long-legged blonde stepped out of the truck and into his arms before they both looked at Eydís and smiled. This was the couple she'd seen briefly upon locating Ulrik and Arkyn at the fair. Ivar was the one Charlotte had pined over in her drunken state. Eydís nodded to the couple. "Ivar. Lucy. It's a pleasure to see you again."

He gently squeezed Lucy and nodded toward the case in Eydís's hands. "Ástin, look, Eydís brought beer."

Lucy laughed and shook her head. "I'll never live down bringing a bottle of wine for my first visit, will I?" Her voice was

light and airy with a subtle accent that sounded a tad like
Jólnir's, minus the Minnesotan influence.

"No yeah. Eydís obviously understands we're just simple
folk in these parts." Ivar answered with a quick kiss to Lucy's
temple. Then he tried to ease the case of beer out of Eydís's
hands. "That's a heavy load ya got there, let me help lighten it."

She shook her head. "Thanks, but I got it."

Ivar simply nodded and retracted his hand, which was weird.
Most men grew huffy when she thwarted their attempts at
chivalry. By contrast, the Drekison men didn't seem to correlate
her self-sufficiency with any insult to their masculinity.

When they reached the side of the house, Ivar ushered both
women up the broad wooden stairs which led around to a
spacious deck at the back. Ulrik was turning steaks at a large
grill and glancing at his phone. Jólnir, Bodil, Arkyn, and another
blond and bearded man who she guessed was the youngest
brother, all leaned against the sturdy railing, gesturing with their
beer bottles and laughing. Two older women, likely the wives,
and a young Asian woman busied themselves setting out enough
food to feed a small country. Then again, seeing how large all the
Drekison men were, this feast might not be enough.

"Hey! The Dragon Lady's here!" Ivar crowed as the
threesome stepped onto the deck.

Eydís's heart stopped and her gut hollowed. How did he
know? How would humans know she came from a dragon clan?
If they knew that, they likely knew she lacked an actual dragon,
that she was defective. Was this a trap? Had they invited her
here to…

Before she could talk herself into a panic, the petite Asian
woman waved her tongs in Ivar's direction and called out to him.
"Eat a bag of dicks, *gwáilóu.*"

She said that as amicably as inquiring about the weather,
and Ivar threw his head back in laughter. The Asian woman—
the Chinese *Dragon Lady*—nodded toward the table. Eydís

wanted to smack herself for assuming Ivar's comment had been meant for her. "I brought shumai. Get some before Ulrik eats it all."

"Eydís, this is—"

"Ivar, why is your ex blowing up my fucking phone?" Ulrik's enraged growl pulled everyone's attention to the grill. He waved the phone at Ivar as if the sheer motion would rid him of the unwanted woman. Eydís cringed inwardly for the part she'd played in encouraging the drunk woman to refocus on the next brother. Ulrik glanced at Eydís and nodded his greeting before glaring at his brother again.

"That woman is more tenacious that a terrier." Arkyn shook his head.

Ulrik snorted. "A terrier I can handle. Charlotte's a fucking plague."

"Could be worse." Ivar shrugged, unconcerned with his brother's struggle as he plucked the case of beer from Eydís's grip before she could react.

"Not sure how." Ulrik muttered as he rubbed the back of his neck and looked skyward as if to beg for patience. Or ideas on where to hide Ivar's body.

"*Jævla fitte.*" Lucy swore out loud and everyone turned, eyes wide in shock at whatever she'd said.

The younger, shorter man clutched his chest dramatically. "Do you kiss your mother with that mouth?"

"No, I kiss *your* mother with this mouth." She shot him a smirk, then stepped toward the two older women, throwing over her shoulder toward Ivar. "I feel sorry for Charlotte, but *hun er en jævla tosk.*"

Both women hugged Lucy like a long, lost daughter, but their attention quickly focused on Eydís. In fact, everyone looked at her. Nerves twisted her gut, which made no sense. She held her own in contentious business meetings all the time, without hesitation or any slip of her self-confidence. So why did the thought of an evening with the Drekison family make her heart race and her palms sweat?

Jólnir stepped from the railing and waved a hand to indicate everyone on the deck. "Welcome to our home, Eydís. We're glad you could join us for dinner."

Ulrik and Ivar argued heatedly, probably about Charlotte, but Eydís couldn't understand many of the words, most of them a jumble of noise. A quick glance proved they weren't near or even looking at each other.

Something similar had happened during this morning's meeting. She would have sworn the four Drekison men were conversing at one point, but their lips had not moved. Was she hearing things? Had she imagined it?

"I second Jólnir's sentiment." Bodil's comment pulled her from the weird sensation of Ulrik and Ivar talking when they couldn't possibly be.

She swallowed past the sudden dryness in her mouth. "Thank you for the invitation. I didn't know what to bring, so I just brought beer."

"Nectar of the gods is always an appropriate gift." Ivar handed her a cold beer, dismissing her attempt to belittle her own contribution. When had she ever sold herself short like that? And why would she do it now?

Jólnir proceeded to introduce her to the family she hadn't already met. His wife was Fröja, the statuesque older woman with thick waves of silvered brown hair. Ivar must get his looks from her. Lucy, whose real name was Lucia, had recently moved from Norway which explained the accent. Bodil's wife was Steph, and her personality was twice as big as she was. The shorter, younger brother was Ty, and his fiancée was the Chinese woman named Wu Lin who spoke like a surfer dude. She owned a popular restaurant in Chinatown, which explained the platter of orange-roe-topped Chinese dumplings amid the Jello-O salad, casserole dishes, and steak sauce bottles on the table.

"Oh, you are so beautiful!" Fröja pulled Eydís into a strong hug as readily as she'd embraced Lucia. Then Fröja pulled back far enough to give her a sly grin. "I heard how you stood up to those *veslinger* during this morning's meeting." She said the foreign word like it was something distasteful before she flashed a triumphant smile and cackled. "I bet they hated every minute of it!"

Steph flanked Eydís and grabbed her hand. "Oh, for sure. Pleeeease tell me you called ol' man Peterson a dimwit. He's about five crayons shy of an eight-pack when it comes to dealing with people."

Eydís was already shaking her head, stunned at how vocal the two women were about their husbands' fellow business associates. But Bodil cut in, pulling Steph toward the table. "No dear, she didn't, at least, not out loud. You can't cure stupid with name-calling. But she knocked him down a few notches."

"She also managed to verbally flay Owen Johnson for being exceptionally bad at his job." Arkyn chuckled, a tone of pride in his voice as he pulled a chair out for Eydís.

"And she pretty much called Larry Olson an idiot." Ulrik bragged as he set a large platter overflowing with juicy steaks on the table.

"N-no." Eydís shook her head harder. "I just—"

"Said what we've all wanted to say for years." Jólnir finished for her, but not with the words she'd intended to say.

"*Uffdah*, you called them all douchebags?" Ivar laughed and fist-bumped a smiling Arkyn.

"My hero." Ty held a hand over his heart as he sat next to Lin at the table.

Eydís sat in an unusual state of mute confusion. They all spoke as if she was unequivocally accepted and already a part of their inner circle. And she'd done nothing to earn it. Not really. All she'd accomplished was hold her own against men who would have automatically given her respect if she had a Y chromosome, and announced a dire situation the family no doubt already knew about.

So, why were they so readily embracing her? And why did it bring her a sense of contentment she'd never before known?

And all the while, her boss's final words played in her head and twisted her gut. *Distract* them. Distract *them*? Maybe she could distract one stupid Larry Olsen. But one Drekison? Let alone the whole Drekison clan? She was good, but that exceeded her skillset. And she lacked the heart to even try.

She was definitely going to lose her job.

CHAPTER NINE

Eydís was overwhelmed. A blind man could see it in the way her gaze flittered around the dinner table like a hummingbird afraid to land. In the way her smile seemed too brittle and her movements too wooden for a casual evening among friends.

A blind man could see the evidence of her unease. Ulrik felt it as if it were his own.

He sat beside her at the table, his thigh and shoulder brushing against hers, electric jolts of awareness with each touch, and he sensed her restraint and confusion poignantly. While everyone else chatted and ate without a care, he merely picked at his meal. Including his two pieces of shumai that were more coveted than *Gungnir*, the spear of Odin.

"Dude, are you okay?" Lin asked through their mental connection. *"I promise I didn't put any ghost peppers in the shumai. That time was a prank."*

Ulrik pushed the food around his plate, a lead weight in his gut where his characteristically endless hunger usually sat. *"I'm okay. I'm just... not very hungry."*

"Everything looks delicious, though." Eydís smiled at Lin as if she'd been included in the private mental conversation. Everyone blinked at her odd interjection. Everyone but Aunt Steph, who wasn't a shifter and thus did not have the ability to participate in their mental chats.

Steph merely beamed at Eydís. "I'm glad you think so, hon. Bodil hunted those elk last week. You should see my kitchen. I'm up to my eyeballs in elk jerky!"

The laughter should have dispelled the awkwardness, but for Ulrik, it continued to hover over dinner. His nerves were on edge as if anticipating an attack. His dragon paced, unsettled and anxious as if also sensing something was wrong but lacking the ability to pinpoint *what*.

"Are you a football fan, Eydís?" Father asked.

"Fair warning before you answer," Arkyn cautioned with a teasing smirk. "You should go ahead and admit you love the Vikings or there'll be no peace at the table tonight."

"Just don't claim to be a cheesehead, and we'll all make it out alive." Ty grabbed for the last shumai on the platter, but Bodil beat him to it and popped it in his mouth with a triumphant grin.

The utter devastation on Ty's face was comical. Under normal conditions, Ulrik might have teased him about it. Instead, he handed over his own two untouched pieces. "Got yer back, bro."

Contrary to his offer's intended effect, now both Ty and Lin looked at him askance.

Eydís still hadn't answered Father's question. Instead, she toyed with the pile of wild rice on her plate, her brows furrowed. When she did answer, her voice soft and hesitant. "Well, honestly, I usually claim to be a fan of whatever team and whatever sport is popular wherever my job takes me."

Her words evoked a sensation of deep emptiness... a

hollowness. Some utter lack of belonging so foreign to Ulrik that it broke his heart and formed a lump in his throat he couldn't swallow. His dragon, too, whined with desperate sorrow.

She glanced around the table. "But really, I just root for whoever plays against New York."

"Ouch. Spoken like a woman done wrong by her team." Lin chuckled.

"I grew up there." Eydís placed her hands in her lap and worried her bottom lip, scowling at the sliver of red Jell-O salad on her plate. When she looked up, she offered a weak chuckle. "There's no love lost there."

Ulrik was shredded by those simple words. And once again, he was not the source of those feelings. Eydís was.

"I grew up in Norway." Lucia's voice quavered, no doubt from the memory of her parents' disappointment that she carried a worthless dragon, when the truth was quite the opposite. "But I didn't find my home—the place where I truly belong—until I came here."

"*Ástin, you can admit it's because of the size of my dick.*" Ivar teased through their mental connection. Everyone but the two humans, Steph and Eydís, snorted in disdain or rolled their eyes at Ivar's typical antics.

Steph blithely cut on her elk steak. But Eydís stared at Ivar like he sported a second head. "Read the room, dude."

He merely blinked with innocence. "What. I didn't say anything."

Eydís huffed and shook her head. "Your dick size making your girlfriend cry is a weird flex, but you do you."

They all stared at her, stunned, for a heartbeat.

"*Eydís, can you hear us?*" Father asked.

"Of course I can." She replied as if that was a silly question. "I mean, I don't always see your lips move. Maybe you're ventriloquists or something, but I hear your voices." She circled a finger in the air as if to indicate she heard the voices in her head. Which made sense... if she were a dragon shifter with their unique ability. But the fact she was a human and could hear their mental communications—

"*So what you're saying is, we should be talking about the size of Ulrik's dick, instead.*" Ivar smiled innocently as Eydís shot him an annoyed glance. Ulrik tensed to throw a punch at his younger brother for being an ass.

"Eydís, dear, I know you may not have fond memories of New York, but I happen to have distant cousins who live there." Mother tucked her hands under her chin and smiled, effectively changing the topic and keeping her sons from a physical altercation. "Did you ever meet any of the Vilulfs?"

Eydís stopped breathing, her beer suspended halfway to her lips. Ulrik felt a surge of grief rise up from his gut, hot and caustic. More than mere acid reflux, this was a wellspring of hurt and yearning coming from Eydís. She knew the Vilulfs. Personally. Yet she shook her head to deny it.

What had the members of the New York dragon clan done to this vibrant woman to cause her such anguish?

"Well, I thought I'd ask anyway." Mother waved away her question as if oblivious to the fact she'd opened a deep, painful wound, and changed the topic. "So, how long will you be with us here in the North Star state?"

"I'll stay until my job is completed." Eydís managed to whisper, her voice strained.

Steph reached out. When Eydís looked at her, Steph squeezed her hand and smiled. "Don't be a stranger, hon. You're always welcome here."

Eydís vaulted to a stand. "I'm sorry I've overstayed my welcome please excuse me." Without waiting for acknowledgment, much less the traditional half-hour Midwest good-bye—she hadn't even slapped her legs and said "Whelp, I'd better go"—she scurried across the deck and down the steps.

Ulrik tensed, every instinct and his own dragon screaming at him to chase after her and hold her until the surge of emotions assaulting her had passed.

"*Leave her be for now. She won't go far.*" Mother directed through their mental connection. She crossed her arms on the table and looked directly at her husband, her demeanor suddenly serious. "*Do you remember the rumor decades ago that the New York clan had a* NeiDreki*?*"

Father nodded and Lucia gasped. "*My father often spoke of their misfortune.*" She turned an apologetic gaze to Bodil, whose children were as human as his wonderful wife. "*Father's words, not mine. And unfortunately, the Council was relieved that the babe had been given up to the state.*"

"*Given away?*" Ivar growled, his red dragon's scales appearing as his skin grew translucent with rage. "*Who gives their child away?*"

Ivar's sneer of disdain was a war cry, and their collective dragons thrashed angrily, ready to do battle. Ulrik's dragon fought to come to the forefront as well, but from a desire to find Eydís and protect her. Hold her. Comfort her.

"*Sending away* NeiDreki *has been a long-standing practice.*" Father's dragon's powers soothed the anger spiking around the table, but his tone made it clear he disagreed with the act. "*The philosophy is it keeps the human children safer than growing up amidst volatile dragons.*"

"*I'm not certain she is entirely human.*" Ulrik frowned as he outlined his reasoning. "*She can hear us in her head. And I can feel her emotions as if they are mine. And she acts like she has a huge beast to back up her brazen attitude.*"

"*Perhaps it is* yuánfèn. *Fate.*" Lin offered. "*Her clan had to reject her so she could find her way to us.*"

"*One man's trash is another man's treasure.*" Ivar shrugged. "*Still. It pisses me off.*"

Steph had stared in the direction of Eydís's exit, her brow

furrowed with worry, until now. She waved an agitated hand toward the rest of the table and clucked her tongue. "Oh, for cripes sake. I know you're all doing your mental chitchat thing, as annoying as that is, and probably deciding that a proper shield maiden doesn't need coddling. But my guess is she's so out of her element she can't find dry land right now. Someone needs to go and save her from drowning."

Ulrik did not hesitate. With a nod to the table, he raced after Eydís, unsure what to do or say when he reached her. *If* he reached her. It was possible she had already driven away.

But she hadn't. She hadn't even reached her car yet. She'd stopped, halfway down the driveway and past the perimeter of lights from the house. Only the half-moon illuminated her, its dim reflection casting her in shadows and wane highlights. She stood still, her back to him, arms at her side and slack, her body trembling from the emotions coursing through her.

Emotions Ulrik was getting very good at sensing, after only one evening. How would he be if they ever made love?

He shook off that thought and unwound the wrap she'd dropped on the ground and settled it over her shoulders, careful to ease into her personal space so he didn't frighten her. She didn't notice at first, too lost in the emotional rabbit hole she'd fallen down. But her fingers twitched against the cashmere, gripping and tugging it closer. Slowly, in increments, she pulled away from the dark abyss she'd stood on the edge of, returning to the present. Returning to him.

Finally, she inhaled, like gasping for air after surfacing. She turned to him, surprise in the depths of her eyes and her cheeks moist with tears she probably didn't know she'd shed.

He cupped her face and dried her tears with his thumbs. "Here, let me wipe this away. Ya got some food on ya." Another fudge of the truth, but better than point out her weakness.

"I did?" Innocent surprise laced her voice and she reached

her fingers to where his spread over her cheeks. She had no idea she'd been crying.

Ulrik paused, her face resting in his palms, her confused gaze on him, like she was still trying to figure out where she was and why. His thumbs arced gently over her smooth cheeks as his body screamed to taste her plump lips. But she'd been drinking. And he didn't want inebriation a possible excuse for dismissing the fireworks he knew in his gut would detonate between them.

Instead, he dropped his hands from her face and stepped back. "Let me have your keys."

That woke her out of her haze. She frowned at him. "Why?"

"You've been drinking. I'm driving you back to your hotel."

Eydís huffed in exasperation and pulled the wrap tighter. "I only had two beers. And you've also been drinking."

"Yeah, but I'm twice your size. Besides, I know these roads like the back of my eyelids. All the twists, turns, deer crossings, and speed traps. I'll get you to your hotel safe and—"

"Or…" She interrupted, pressing a single fingertip to his mouth to halt his words. "You're just full of hooey and looking for a way to spend more time with me."

He smiled. It had taken her a moment, but she'd finally called him on his bullshit. She was back to baseline, that boulder of memories and emotions crushing her during dinner rolled away so she could breathe again. Dare he attribute it to his touch?

"Can't we both be right?" He wrapped his hand around hers and eased it away from his mouth, wondering how she'd react if he ran his tongue along the length of her finger.

Instead of flirting back, she sighed, her shoulders drooping as if under a great weight. But not the overwhelming weight she'd struggled with during dinner. This was different.

She looked around the darkness, searching for an answer to some unspoken question. When she finally met his gaze, her expression resembled the one she had this morning when she'd warned Father against trusting anyone. "Ulrik, we're not friends. We can't be friendly. You know that, right?"

He snorted. "Why, because we're business competitors? Eydís, all the men in the meeting this morning are Drekison Logging competition. Hell, I bowl in a league with half of them. Being competitors doesn't mean we can't be civil."

"Civil? You mean, like, infiltrating your private company property and releasing thousands of Pine Mountain beetles in an effort to disable your business? That kind of civil? How's that working for you?"

He rested his hand on his hip and scratched his beard with the other. There she was again, not pulling her punches. But he couldn't hold it against her because she hadn't said anything that wasn't true. "Ya got me there, and I don't know what to tell ya except that doesn't mean *I* have to be uncivil. At least until we know who is actually doing it. Now, how about those keys so I can drive you safely back to your hotel?"

Eydís gaped at him, mouth slack, for several blinks before she sighed in defeat and tossed her rental car keys at him, shaking her head as she got in the passenger side before he could open the door for her. Even so, he waited patiently for her to get situated, then closed the door for her. Before she could work up a huff over his chivalry, he rounded the front of the car and slid into the driver's seat.

"Sorðinn!" He cursed as his knees hit the dash and the automatic gear shift in the center console gouged his ribs. He'd forgotten she was short and hadn't adjusted the seat before folding himself in half. He was nearly shoe-horned in already, so leaned forward to reach the lever to slide the seat back, dashing his forehead on the rearview mirror for his effort. Then his hand hit the steering wheel tilt lever, and it dropped, smashing his crotch. He grunted, wheezing to catch the breath shoved out his lungs.

Fuck, battling *Niðhöggr* hadn't been this painful or lasted this long. When he finally got the seat in position and his seat belt buckled, he heard the laughter Eydís tried to hide behind the hand clamped over her mouth. He scowled at her, but that only made her laugh harder, her eye glittering and her face euphoric with humor.

Well, he'd wanted to help dispel her anguish. Mission accomplished.

"Sorry, not sorry for laughing at you." She managed to choke out.

"That was almost enough to get me into Valhalla." He smiled at her, not minding that she laughed at his expense because it was so much better than what she'd suffered during dinner.

Eydís placed a hand over her heart. "My hero."

Ulrik started the car and put it in Drive, then winked at her. "Careful. That sounds like something a friend would say."

She didn't respond. Instead, she dropped her gaze to her lap, nibbled her bottom lip, and stared out the window as he drove. A comfortable silence filled the car, but he needed more. His parent's words about the New York clan and *NeiDreki* rang in his head. Maybe that hadn't been Eydís they remembered, but he desperately wanted her to know as much about his family as he could share. As if that familiarity could fill whatever void she had.

So he talked.

He talked about how his parents and Uncle Bodil had moved to Minnesota from Norway. How Aunt Steph and Bodil had met. How they were expecting their first grandchild and Ulrik and his brothers competed over who would be the favorite Uncle-cousin, each of them not-so-secretly buying cuter clothes and more expensive toys than the last. How Ty had moved to LA and teased that he'd fallen in love with Lin because of her red bean buns. How competitive winter ice fishing was between the brothers—

"What about you?" Eydís murmured as he pulled into the hotel parking lot.

He blinked at her. "What do you mean? I'm right in there with the rest of them. We usually come to blows over whether the winner is determined by size or quantity of fish caught."

"You mean quality never gets considered?" She snorted.

She wasn't talking about fish. "What, you don't think size is important?"

"To a certain extent, size matters." She nibbled her lips and he wanted to replace her teeth with his own. "But if the fisherman doesn't know how to handle his pole, size alone won't help him catch anything."

She definitely wasn't talking about fish. Eydís faced him. "So what about you?" she asked again.

"Oh, I know how to handle my pole." That wasn't the answer to her question, but he wasn't sure what she wanted. The air in the car grew thick with their breaths and a sense of anticipation. "At least, none of the fish have complained."

"Fish usually don't complain. They just stop biting." Her smile was melancholy, and she fidgeted with the hem of her sundress where it rested atop her knee. "But that's not what I meant. You spent the last twenty minutes telling me all about your family. But barely told me anything about yourself."

She smoothed her skirt over her shapely thighs.

"So…" her voice dropped to a throaty whisper he felt all the way to his cock. "What about you?"

He cleared his throat and took a moment to collect his thoughts. What could he tell her? What did he want her to know? What did she want to hear? He shrugged. "Well, Arkyn is the heir. Ivar oversees the construction side of the business with Uncle Bodil. Ty has his own life in California with Lin. And I'm… I'm just the spare. The redundancy."

"The spare? You mean, like Prince Henry and William?"

He pursed his lips to consider the comparison, but shook his head. "More like the backup or the contingency plan? The support?"

Ulrik chuckled and scraped a hand down his face. "That's not accurate, either. I'm just... I'll always ever be number two. The second-born. The second choice. Does that make sense?" He shrugged, as if it didn't matter, and usually it didn't. But there had been times in his life the truth had rankled. When he stood in the office with Father and Arkyn, silently watching them mastermind corporate strategies without asking for his input. When out at the bars, with women who'd chosen him simply because Arkyn had already picked his evening's hookup. Always the athletic supporter to Arkyn's star power; the assist to Arkyn's goals. Always taking orders but never giving them.

He pulled his thoughts back to the beautiful woman in this car. He palmed her face like he had back at the house. Not to comfort her but because he could no longer keep away from her. He ran his thumb along her plump bottom lip. Odin's beard he wanted her. Wanted to taste her. The inches separating them in this car were painful; he wanted her so flush against his own body, their lungs shared the same molecules of air. Wanted his hands and his mouth all over her silky skin.

A low moan escaped her lips, her pupils wide with desire, her breaths shallow and swift. She licked her lips. "Ulrik, for what it's worth, you've always been my first choice."

She kissed him. She fisted his shirt and half-pulled him toward her, half-leveraged his size to haul herself to his lap until they were twisted and splayed across the console, her tongue in his mouth and her soft mews in his ears.

Fireworks exploded in his head. He knew they would. By the Allfather, she tasted of mead, the heady combination of honey and victory. He was drunk on her lips. He wrapped his arms around her, pulling her against his chest, her full breasts and pebbled nipples marking him as hers. His hands exploring her curves, threading through her hair and roaming from her slender waist, over the swell of her hips and curve of her lush ass to her luscious thighs. Her own fingers gripped his hair and clawed at his shoulders. All the while their tongues danced and their breaths mingled. His deep moans harmonized with her high, breathy sighs.

Eydís twisted, pushing further onto his lap, but her back hit the steering wheel. The car's horn blared, shocking them back to reality. She scrabbled back to her own seat, clasping the edges like she might otherwise fall out, her eyes wide and frantic, her breaths coming in gulps.

Ulrik wasn't much better, wanting to rip the offending steering wheel out so he could pull her back onto his lap and continue where they'd left off. His erection strained against his zipper, and his fingertips tingled, desperate to explore the flesh hidden by her clothes.

But the pop-up storm of lust and desire swirling around them had passed. Reality whooshed in, heralded by the jarring car horn and following the ever-present truth: They couldn't be friendly, because they were corporate enemies.

Eydís smoothed her hair and her clothes in an effort to regain her composure. He still struggled to wrangle his desire into submission—his body strained to pick up where they'd left off—when she cleared her throat and opened her door. Her lips were swollen from his kisses, but she pursed them together as if that would undo an unpleasant memory. She held out her hand for the car fob. "Thank you for driving me to my hotel. I hope it's not too much trouble for you to get a ride home."

Without a word, because she hadn't invited him to her room and he didn't trust himself not to beg her to come back to the circle of his arms, he handed her the fob and unfolded himself from the driver's seat. Their recent intimacy still fresh in his mind and the flavor of her tongue lingering on his, he stood and looked at her over the car's roof, giving her what he hoped was a reassuring smile. "I'll be fine, Eydís. I hope you enjoyed your evening, and wish you a good night's sleep."

Not waiting for her to respond, he headed toward the darkness beyond the parking lot lights to shift and fly home. She didn't call him back. And he didn't know whether to be relieved or disappointed.

CHAPTER TEN

U lrik's parting words last night had been to wish her a good night's sleep. As if that was possible. Eydís had tossed and turned all night thinking about him and the World's Hottest Kiss—the one she'd walked away from like an idiot— and what he must think of her being such a dick-tease-ice-princess.

But she couldn't tell her boss any of that. Not that he'd let her get a word in during this morning's micromanage-your-capable-employees-to-death-by-yelling-obscenities-at-them phone call.

Her only saving grace was the fact she'd grabbed an armful of coffees in the drive-thru before having to park in the coffee shop's lot to accept the call. Without that massive caffeine intake, she might snap. Or drive all the way back to the home office just to bitch slap him.

"So you had dinner with the entire Drekison family last night, and didn't manage to learn a single. Fucking. Bit. Of. Useful. Information." Frank's voice was so low and growly she could practically hear the froth on his dentures.

And how did he know she'd had dinner with the Drekisons? That was information she had not yet shared.

"It was a family dinner, not a business dinner. There were wives and girlfriends there, and gleaning corporate secrets had not been on the menu." She took a long drink of her venti to halt the sass in her voice. She was too tired to be taken to task for shit she hadn't accomplished on her boss's super-secret Eydís-To-Do-But-Don't-Tell-Her list. That was his right as her employer, so she had to grin and bear it. Well, she had to bear it. If she wanted to keep her job.

She took another swallow of coffee, because that last point was feeling pretty questionable at the moment.

"So, how soon can I expect the Drekisons to cave?"

There was no way her boss was that dense.

"Frank, as I told you barely twelve hours ago, the Drekisons are in no way concerned about their beetle infestation. A buy-out offer at this point is moot."

"I'm not talking a buy-out offer, you stupid bitch!" His scream stabbed her ears drums. And she glanced around the parking lot to make sure no one passing by had heard through the glass and metal of her rental car. "When are they going to crumble under your rape charges and sell out to me?"

She nearly dropped her venti in her lap. "Rape charges? Why would I accuse anyone of rape?"

The line was so quiet, she thought she'd gone deaf. Then Frank's voice, as low and dangerous as a rattlesnake, slithered through the air. "Because the Drekisons plied you with alcohol during dinner and the second son drove you back to your hotel room and raped you while you were too drunk to resist."

Her heart stopped and her blood iced over. There was so much wrong with that one statement, not the least of which was the abhorrent fact he actually wanted her to claim she'd been raped. But he'd already concocted a false narrative to back it up... with a story weirdly close to the actual events, minus all the drama. She had imbibed alcohol, the second son had driven her to her hotel room, and they'd been hot and heavy in her car for a several minutes. Aside from the fact the entire evening had been safe and consensual, the basic details of Frank's story aligned way too specifically to the actual events. Especially for someone several states away whose only insider knowledge should be what she'd reported to him.

When she found her voice, she tried to laugh off his ridiculous accusation. "Frank, are you off your meds? I wasn't drunk and he didn't rape me. We didn't have sex. Those would be empty allegations and unprovable."

"I. Don't. Care." Frank's voice rose in volume like an erupting volcano. "Or do I have to *come down there and DO EVERYTHING MYSELF?*"

Eydís grabbed the phone from her dash and screamed back. "Good idea. *You come here and FUCK A DREKISON BROTHER!*"

She ended the call and turned the phone off, flinging it across the car. Her chest heaved and her head throbbed and tears burned her eyes. She rested her head against the steering wheel. The same traitorous one that had ended her panty-melting make-out session with Ulrik last night. The session she'd initiated because she couldn't stand another moment longing to kiss him. Even now, her body heated at the thought of being pressed against his muscles, his hands and tongue exploring her like she was a wondrous new adventure.

And somehow, that amazing kiss was getting twisted in an insidious manner by her boss. What kind of fucked up world was this? This was beyond shady. This was illegal. Wrong. Immoral. Absolutely... unconscionable.

Had Frank always been this unhinged?

She needed to tell someone about this. Needed to come clean about what Frank had said so he couldn't throw her under the bus. She had to protect herself. She had to protect the Drekisons. She had to—

A knock on her window made her jump. A man on the other side smiled and waved at her. Someone from yesterday's meeting. One of the Peterson grandsons, but she couldn't remember his name. She was in no mood to make nice, but threw on her mantle of professionalism anyway and rolled her window down.

"Hey howdy." The man shoved his face too close and she jerked back with a frown. Personal space, much? "Ope, didn't mean to scare ya. Just saw ya sittin' here and thought I'd be neighborly and say hi."

She raised the car window enough he flinched back. Then she managed a smile. "Well, thank you for the thought. You have a good day."

He plunked his hand over the edge of the window as if to stop her from driving away. She was tempted to hit the window button and watch it rise up until it pinched his fingers. Under normal circumstances, she would have, all the while giving him her best *you're a dumbass* look. But knowing he was a business competitor of the Drekisons, which made him in some small-town convoluted sense their business *associate*, and could very well be on Ulrik's damn bowling league team stalled her hand. She merely looked at him expectantly.

"You might not remember me from yesterday's meeting, but I'm Chad Peterson of Peterson and Sons Lumber." The open, hopeful expression on his face made her regret her bitchy thoughts. He was maybe early thirties, no ring on his finger, and not bad looking. He was no Drekison brother, but very few men were.

And comparing him to Ulrik wasn't fair. Eydís sighed and forced a smile on her face. "Yes, Chad. I remember you."

He beamed as if she'd agreed to go to prom with him. But then he crossed his arms against her door and leaned closer, as if to share a secret. He glanced surreptitiously around before lowering his voice. "So, how's the mission going?"

His actions, combined with her recent, er, *chat,* with her boss, tipped her scales immediately to *paranoid.* "Mission?"

He blinked at her. "Yeah, the mission. You know, to find whoever sabotaged the Drekisons and stop the infestation." He huffed a laugh. "Good gravy, what did you think I meant?"

Her patience was nonexistent, and her smile no doubt said as much. "Well, it's only been one day, and I've made about as much progress as all of you made in the last three weeks."

He seemed not to notice the bite of sarcasm in her voice. "Ya know, if you wanted to survey Peterson lands for infestation, I'd be happy to escort you."

His offer was innocent enough, but she couldn't shake the creep factor. Follow him out to the middle of unknown terrain with nothing but her wit and her mouth? That didn't sound ominous or anything.

"Thanks for the offer, Chad. But I was told all the companies already surveyed their lands. So that would be a waste of both my time and talent."

Flashing him her coldest smile, she hit the Up switch on the window and mouthed her good-bye as she backed the car out of the space. If any of Chad's body parts got in the way, well, that was on him because she no longer had any fucks to give.

Without a plan for where to go, except away from Chad, she drove. Drove out of the town and along the sparsely populated roads. On autopilot while her brain drew blanks for how to deal with anything that had happened since she'd arrived. The past few days were a personal nightmare. Like Fate had finally washed its hands of her and had chucked her into Midwest Hell. This was worse than any Groundhog Day continual do-over. This was a new challenge and a new unwinnable situation each day, compounding frustration until she wanted to scream.

And she was only on day four.

When she finally stopped driving, she found herself at the Drekison's office. Somehow, her car or her muscles had known to come here, even though this was the last place she should be. She was being used as the instrument for their disgrace and demise, and yet she didn't know where else to go for comfort or help.

This family was the only bright spot in her nightmare.

Parking next to Ulrik's truck, she grabbed her carrier of coffees and met him halfway as he came out to greet her.

"Eydís, it's a pleasure to see you here." If he was shocked she'd arrived unannounced and uninvited, he didn't show it. Instead, he lifted the carrier out of her hands before she could reject his assistance, and placed a warm, comforting hand at the small of her back to usher her into the office.

Stepping into the log cabin office was better than any spa day. Her tension melted away and every inhale relaxed and invigorated her cells, so different than when she'd entered yesterday. Maybe they piped in weed or vaporized heroine. All she knew was this place felt like coming home.

A home she'd never had.

"Come this way. I think you'll like the view." His voice was in her ear and his warmth pressed against her side. If he was feeling awkward after she'd thrown herself at him last night, he didn't show it. He merely guided her out a sliding glass door to the cozy back deck which boasted a few Adirondack chairs and a glorious vista of the Drekison forests sloping away from the cabin.

So enchanted by the gently rolling hills of green pine trees punctuated with orange and yellow deciduous trees, she barely noticed as he tucked a blanket around her to stave off the morning chill and handed her coffee in a ceramic mug.

When he settled in the chair next to hers, she smiled at him. "You're right. I do like the view." She meant the trees, but the way he filled out his plaid flannel lent her words a double meaning. He'd pulled his hair back into a low ponytail and a simple silver rune pendant dangled from a leather strap around his neck. She'd barely eaten any dinner and had skipped breakfast, and Ulrik Drekison looked like a total snack.

Her mouth watered, remembering how delicious his kisses were.

His smile was warm and welcoming. If he was remembering their passionate embrace last night, he didn't show it. That should bother her, but it didn't. One of them needed to have their head on straight. "Eydís, you seem to be a little distracted. Last night as well. Is there anything I can help you with?"

If only he could. If only she could run to his arms and let him protect her from all the big meanies in her life. But she was a grown-ass woman and needed to save herself. She curled her legs up and leaned against the armrest, taking a long sip of coffee from her mug. Somehow, it tasted better than any cardboard go-cup coffee, no matter how fancy the coffee house.

She glanced around. "Where are Arkyn and your father?"

"They had a meeting with a pallet company that might be interested in the raw lumber from our dead trees. I stayed back to man the fort." He rested an ankle on his knee and cupped his coffee mug.

Always second in command. She remembered his confession from last night and frowned at the fact that, once again, he was left out. "Does that upset you? To not be included in the meeting?"

He considered her question, then shook his head. "I'm always welcome to tag along. I just… thought it important I stayed here instead. Gut feel, ya know."

"What? Like you knew I was going to show up?"

"No. Just…" He pursed his lips as if trying to find the words to explain. He finally shrugged and offered her a lopsided smile. "I felt a disturbance in The Force, I guess. Maybe I did somehow know you would show up."

"Glad one of us did." She murmured and chewed her bottom lip. It was like Fate wanted to throw the two of them together. Or her subconscious. Maybe she hadn't actually bought all that coffee just for herself. But if her boss had his way, being here with Ulrik was a recipe for disaster.

She couldn't do that to him. To his family. "We shouldn't be here alone."

He chuckled at her cautionary tone. "Why? You gonna throw yourself at me again? I didn't hate it, ya know."

Here it was. The moment she needed to come clean. He needed to know her boss's evil plan, so he could defend against it. Against her. So he could warn his family and they could give her wide berth so no one could claim anything untoward going on.

Her heart cringed at having to say good-bye when she'd barely said hello.

"*So Eydís, what are your plans?*"

She blinked as his simple question rang directly in her head like a gong, discordant with the direction of her morose thoughts. Her heart dropped to her gut. Did he know about her orders to ruin Drekisons Logging? Or was he pulling a Chad Peterson and pretending to mean her plan for finding the saboteur?

He looked directly at her from over the top of his coffee mug as he took a sip. "Surely you have plans for your life." He clarified, concern twisting his smile. His voice in her ears rather than her head this time.

Something about that comment made her itch to stand up and move. Walk around. Run. Drive away and fly somewhere. It was an unpleasant nomadic impulse brought on by Ulrik's simple question. Why would it unlock such a boiling wellspring of anxiety unrelated to the fear her boss had already unleashed? She cleared her throat and focused on answering, when she really wanted to scream and flee. "Um, well, I plan to continue working for Hilda Timbers. Maybe meet someone. Or, probably stay single. Maybe get a dog if I can ever stop traveling for work." A dog that looked at her with soft, adoring, puppy dog eyes like how Ulrik currently looked at her.

Ulrik set his mug on the small table between their chairs and faced her. "Eydís, those are possibilities, not plans. Surely you have a goal or a direction. We're people; we require action. Forward momentum."

"Oh believe me, I have plenty of action and movement in my life."

"*Forward* movement. Toward a goal you've given yourself, not one you've been given by someone else. If we aren't personally invested in our own future, then our heart isn't in our present."

It was her turn to shrug, as if this conversation wasn't shredding her. "What if the goals given by others align with my own?"

Well, they had aligned until yesterday.

"You mean your goal of working for Hilda? Congrats, you've accomplished it. Now what?"

"Can't I simply want to maintain that goal?"

Why would she want to? Ulrik was poking a festering wound with his comments, and her agitation grew.

Or maybe she wasn't ready for this intense introspection.

He shook his head. "Maintaining a goal we've already accomplished isn't forward progress. You have to keep moving."

"I've moved all my life." She snapped at him. "Maybe I want to stop moving for a bit."

He gazed at her for a few heartbeats, his expression unreadable. Then he sat back in his seat and faced the woods around them. She stared into the depths of her coffee as if she could find answers there.

When he spoke, his voice was tender, like a mental caress. "*People aren't meant to be islands, ya know, even if they are goddesses.*" She blinked at his reference to the meaning of her name. "We're like this forest." He waved his arm to indicate all the trees visible from the office's back desk. "We grow together, and reach our roots into the earth to intertwine with the roots of others around us. Our roots—our community—give us strength and support and make us stronger than a solitary tree."

Anger burst in her chest. Who the fuck was he to lecture her about her life? She sneered. "Nice analogy. Roots also keep you stagnant. They keep you in one place so you never think to leave. Because if you never see what the world has to offer, you'll never know you're not happy where you've been planted. Community? Support? Like how one of your competitors is trying to destroy your business?"

She couldn't stop the venom in her voice, but he didn't seem riled by it. Instead of matching her energy, he merely turned to her with a pointed look. "Has your untethered, self-reliant existence brought you contentment? Happiness? Love?"

She bit her lip, refusing to answer. She'd never known any of those things. Maybe she wasn't meant to. Maybe they were merely false constructs of society intended to keep the sheep under control.

Ulrik didn't let up. "Eydís, not having any roots means outside influences can blow you about at their whims. Like tumbleweed. You think you're in charge of your life, but you're not."

"Neither are you, and yet you have such deep roots." Ouch, that was a low blow, but he wasn't pulling his punches either.

"I often wonder if there is something more I should be doing with my life." He readily admitted, deflating her verbal victory. "But *I* am still the one in control of that destiny. No one else."

This was the most frustrating fight ever. Ulrik didn't back down or concede, but merely deflected each of her verbal blows without taking any nasty shots of his own. What kind of maniac remained so calm in situations like these? She set her coffee mug down next to his with enough force to slosh some over the edge.

"So, just because you've had neither the desire nor the courage to venture out into the world on your own, the rest of us are dumbasses for not *setting down roots*. Like we're vagrant Spanish Moss?"

"If you prefer a more adventurous, carefree lifestyle, that's a choice, not an indicator of intelligence." He leaned toward her as if to punctuate the gravity of his tone. "But this past year has shown me with unquestionable clarity how important our connections to one another are. Family. Friends. Community. Together, we are powerful and undefeatable."

Eydís stood, vibrating with the urge to punch something. "Thank you for your hospitality. I'll take my leave now."

She marched past him and beelined through the office to the front door. If this emotional roller coaster was what it meant to be part of a family—of a community—she'd gladly nope the fuck out of that shit.

CHAPTER ELEVEN

"Running away again, huh?" Ulrik's threw the taunt out, hoping it would snare Eydís long enough he could talk her off her emotional precipice. Which was funny. Because all his stupid talk is what had brought her to that point. "Did a little meaningful conversation scare you that much?"

She stopped, her hand on the front door handle, and whirled on him. Her chest heaved with rage and her eyes flashed with fire. "Meaningful conversation? I think you mean *unprovoked criticism.*"

He canted his head. "I spoke about community and setting down roots. How is *that* criticism?"

"It's clear you're judging my life's choices and found them lacking. I don't need to sit and listen to you pretend to be better than me."

"Yesterday, you held your own against a room full of men judging you and finding you lacking, and you didn't stomp away in a huff. You didn't even flinch." He stepped toward her like one might approach a rabid wild animal. "But I talk about home and roots and being a *part* of something bigger than we as mere individuals, and suddenly that's too much to handle."

"I stood up to those men yesterday because that is the nature of our business." She threw her shoulders back and straightened to her full height, as if she could physically intimidate him. All it did was push her breasts toward him and damn if that wasn't distracting. "I'm walking away from you because I can."

"You're walking away from me because you want me, and it terrifies you."

Like when playing Bridge with the family, he threw out his strongest card. Hopefully, it was enough to trump her outrage.

Her resulting laugh was high and brittle. And she wouldn't meet his gaze. "Th-that most certainly is not the case."

"That fake laugh says otherwise." He stopped in front of her. If he pushed her too hard, she could easily step through the office entrance and be gone. "Eydís, you don't strike me as someone afraid to face the truth or call a spade a spade."

She glared at him and he braced for another biting retort. Instead, her shoulders sank as if she could no longer sustain those strong emotions. She huffed a laugh as she shook her head. "Look, I'm sure you're very popular with the ladies around these parts. I get it. I've seen the competition, and it's like painting a wild turkey white and calling it a swan. But just because you're one of the hottest men around, doesn't mean every single woman wants to jump you."

Ouch. She'd hit below the belt on that one and probably didn't realize it. Her comment hadn't been malicious. Most women did prefer Arkyn to him. But the truth still stung. However, Eydís had, in fact, jumped him last night, although he wouldn't be cad enough to point out that detail. "You're right."

She seemed shocked by his easy agreement.

"My brothers and I have never lacked for female attention, and I've never had to work for it." He leaned in, framing her torso with his hands gripping the push bar, so close he could smell the sultry mix of bergamot and vanilla dabbed on her pulse points. "But that has no bearing on the fact that I want you."

"You…" She swallowed hard and licked her lips. "You just think you do, because I'm a novelty. A challenge. Because I'm not throwing myself at you."

Okay, that was twice she'd made that claim. He slanted her a knowing smirk. Guilt creased her forehead and she worried her lips. She knew full well she'd lied.

"Yes, you challenge me, but that's not what makes you so irresistible." He dipped his head, his facial hair tickling along her jawline and neck as he inhaled her intoxicating scent. His lips replaced his whiskers, tracing along the sensitive lines of her neck and the shell of her ears. Her breath hitched and her nipples pebbled in his peripheral.

He threaded his fingers through the silky strands of her hair as his tongue followed his lips. Then he fisted her hair and pulled her head back, licking the sensitive spots on her throat. Her eyes fluttered shut and her exhale hitched. As he had already a few times this morning, he spoke to her using his shifter's mental communication. "*I want you, Eydis. More than any woman I've ever known. But if you truly don't desire me, tell me now and I will stop.*"

Don't fucking stop!

He stifled a moan at her internal scream. She may not have meant for him to hear that mental thought, but the desperation in her tone, and the way her fingers clutched at him were all the green light he needed. He wrapped his other arm around her waist, tugging her against his erection and the friction made them both moan. Her thighs parted as if in invitation and he rolled his hips, thrusting against her core, hating, yet grateful for, the layers of clothes between them.

He pulled away to look in her face, her pupils wide in her green eyes. His tongue swiped across his lips, eager to taste her. His breathing as erratic as hers.

"I—" She inhaled and looked at him. He sensed her internal struggle between her desire and a protectiveness he didn't understand. "I... I shouldn't want you. I'm no good for you. I'm not girlfriend material and I'll just make you miserable."

If she could honestly claim she had no desire to be with him, he would walk away and bother her no more. But those weren't her words, and this lame excuse that she wasn't good for him? He'd be the judge of that. And dragon shifters were excellent judges of character.

"You shouldn't want me, but you do?" He brushed his fingertips over her cheekbone and tucked a strand of hair behind her ear. "Thank Christ for that, because I've wanted you since the first moment I saw you."

Slowly, giving her one last chance to stop him, he lowered his head until he finally pressed his lips to hers.

Fireworks.

Glittering shards of light exploded in his head, brighter than the Fourth of July, raining sizzling tendrils down his body to his cock, catching his nerve endings ablaze like a dry, desperate forest. His passion was tinder sparked by her moan as she arched against him, enflamed by the heated Santa Ana winds of their kiss. And that was a horrible analogy, but what could he expect when ninety percent of his blood rushed away from his brain to other areas of his body? Odin's beard, she was a feast for the halls of Valhalla.

Like a forest fire, need raged through their limbs. She clawed at his shirt, wrapping her leg around his thigh, lifting to her tiptoes to grind against his erection through their clothes. Ulrik palmed her ass, squeezing and lifting her higher against his body. She wrapped her legs around his waist while his cock continued to knock insistently at the apex of her thighs. Their tongues danced and their hips rocked and damn these clothes why couldn't he wish them away. He wanted her naked and riding his cock so he could douse this inferno of need scraping at his raw nerves and turning him into a rutting creature as mindless as she.

Their entwined bodies knocked against the office front door, the unlocked entrance pulsing with each thrust of his hips.

"*Oh sweet lítill fura. I can't get enough of you.*" Ulrik growled the thought to her as he planted hungry, possessive kisses along her neck and collarbone, his hands plumping and squeezing her ass. "*You burn so fierce, Eydís. Like a firestorm. Like the sun. You're going to turn me to ash, and I'll love every moment of it.*"

She arched her back, her moans more erratic as her pleasure mounted. She was going to come and they'd done nothing more than kiss and dry hump. How amazing would it be if they were ever skin-to-skin? "Ulrik." Her low moan drew out his name as the swell of her climax crested.

"*Ulrik.*" Her voice in his head. No, not her voice. Arkyn's? Why would—

"Fuck!" She screamed, but not from pleasure. Urlik looked up to see both his brother and father standing on the outside of the Drekison office front door. Odin only knew how much they'd seen, and he thanked the Allfather he and Eydís hadn't shed any clothing.

But that knowledge wouldn't be any relief for the woman in his arms who already pushed at him to extricate herself from his embrace. He gently released her so she wouldn't fall or topple, but as soon as her feet hit the floor, she was out the door, her hand covering her face and muttering a tearful apology to Arkyn and Father as she raced to her car.

And not a backward glance to Ulrik, who still burned to have her back in his arms.

His family was the ultimate cock block.

"I'm so sorry. We didn't realize until we were right there." Arkyn's expression and tone carried his regret.

Ulrik threaded his trembling fingers through the locks of hair that had come loose from its band. His arousal morphed into a need for action. He had to go after Eydís. Had to tell her—

"Leave her be." Father clamped a hand on his shoulders. "She'll be fine. She's just embarrassed."

He'd never questioned his father's advice before. But at the moment, it seemed insufficient for the situation. "No offense, but if that were Mother, you'd go after her. I will do the same for Eydís."

Father squeezed his shoulder and nodded his understanding. "You do what you need to, son."

～

Ulrik parked his car in his parent's side yard. He'd spent nearly an hour trying to track Eydís, but she'd disappeared like the morning mist. He wasn't ready to return to the office. So, had sought out his mother.

He walked through the back door of the house he'd grown up in, like he'd done a million times before. Mother took one look from where she was cutting vegetables and stopped immediately, grabbing the coffee pot and nodding toward the cozy breakfast table. Her throne. How many soul-bearing conversations had she had with her husband and sons over the years? Today, it was his turn.

By the Allfather, he needed it.

"What's going on with Eydís?" Mother cut right to the heart of it. When he slanted her a surprised look, she shrugged. "I'm a mother of boys. I know that girl-trouble look."

Ulrik's chuckle was without humor as he slumped onto a chair and plucked a *skillingsboller* from the plate next to his coffee mug. The pastry's familiar butter, cinnamon sugar, and warm cardamom spice soothed like a familiar blanket. Perhaps Eydís could also benefit from a coffee talk with Mother. Maybe he should suggest it when he finally found her.

"Eydís stopped by the office while I was there alone." Ulrik explained while Mother waited patiently across the table from him, sipping from her own cup of coffee. "She was upset, but we ended up arguing over something slight. Or… maybe not so slight. She accused me of criticizing her, although I sensed it was just an excuse to keep me from knowing what truly bothered her. But then we ended up…"

What could he say? Kissing? Making out? Dry humping? Nothing seemed to accurately describe those moments in each other's arms.

Mother chuckled. "You can say *in the throes of passion.* Unless you two went straight to whips and chains, your father and I have done it, so no need to be coy or embarrassed."

Ulrik nearly choked on his coffee. Whips and chains and his parents being intimate were not concepts that should be in the same sentence. "That's a mental image I didn't need, Mother."

"Don't hesitate with your words next time." She shrugged, an unrepentant smile on her lips. "I didn't raise my sons to be timid."

Fair enough. He cleared his throat and began again. "We were in throes of passion. Against the office front door. And Father and Arkyn arrived right when Eydís… well, *arrived* as well. They saw. She freaked. And I don't know what to do to rectify her embarrassment."

"She would likely tell you she is okay. Because she's a confident, self-reliant woman."

He nodded. Then shook his head. "So why do I get the feeling it's an act? She is so capable, yet her insistence on being independence and self-sufficient seems forced. Distrustful. Like if she says it enough, she'll actually believe it."

"Maybe she's never had anyone she could rely on to help her. So she's been forced to become that for herself." Mother's soft-spoken suggestion was a clanging horn in his head.

Ulrik shot to his feet and paced the kitchen, trying to give voice to his thoughts as they flopped around his brain like fish during the spring spawn. "Why do I believe there's more to her than the hard-ass businesswoman she shows the world? Why do I need to prove to her she can be soft and it's not a weakness? She only has a limited time here, and I can't break through her armor or secure her feelings in just a few days. Not if she's going to refuse to see. And why does she call to me, to my dragon, like she does? It's this… steel cable yanking me in her direction. I can't fight it. I can't ignore it. We are both so finely attuned to her. And yet so clueless and useless to help her."

Mother chuckled like he'd spewed a comedy routine. He whirled on her, shocked she'd take his jumbled worries so lightly. She shook her head and patted the table to bring him back to his seat. When he complied, she gripped his hand in hers, her strength lending her words weight. "Ulrik, all your life, you have gravitated toward the broken. Injured birds. Shelter animals. People in pain. Your dragon's power might be wood, but yours is your heart. You live with it open and welcoming for the weary and wary."

"You make me sound like the Statue of Liberty, Mother." He grumbled. He hadn't been raised to be a doormat, but here his own mother accused him of just that.

She slapped his hand lightly. "It's a good thing, *drengr*. You make us all better people because we know we have a safe place to land in your heart."

How was that a good thing? His mother rarely angered him, but this declaration was insulting. "I'm a warrior, Mother. The same as my brothers."

"I never said you weren't." She made a dismissive sound and waved his concerns away. "You mistake having an open heart for weakness."

Ulrik opened his mouth to speak, but Ivar's voice through their mental connection interrupted. "*So, Ulrik. Have you fucked Eydís yet?*"

"Eldhúsfífl, *that's none of your business!*" Ulrik growled in response.

"*But it is* our *business.*" Ivar explained calmly. "*I passed Chad Peterson in town. He crowed about Drekison woods being sold for pennies and developed into a middle-income subdivision.* After *Miss Helvig fucks you.*"

A pause, then laughter rang through the family mental connection, with the noted exception of Ulrik and Mother.

Ty teased. "*How bad of a lay does one have to be to give up company land as compensation?*"

"*Maybe Eydís is just that good of a lay.*" Lin snorted.

"*Did Chad happen to say how he came by this information?*" Bodil asked.

The shrug was clear in Ivar's voice. "*He merely claimed insider knowledge and a secret partnership with Hilda.*"

"*Is Chad really that stupid as to show his hand like this?*" Lucia's voice was filled with disbelief.

All the Drekisons confirmed in unison: Chad Peterson was really that stupid. Stupid and greedy, and obviously willing to undo years of community cooperation.

Ulrik blinked at this new bit of information. Eydís was supposed to fuck him, and that would somehow ruin his family's company? Perhaps that explained why she was so hot and cold with him. If he'd been given such unsavory orders, he'd be similarly tormented, especially if he was as attracted to the person as he senses Eydís was to him.

Mother stood and cleared the coffee mugs. "You get back to the office, dear. And when you find where Eydís is, let me know. I'll pay her a visit and offer her a bit of motherly advice."

"Don't be too hard on her." He asked, frowning at his hands, his emotions swirling. "My gut tells me she's backed into a corner. Maybe has been for a long time."

CHAPTER TWELVE

E ydís drove around blindly for hours. She'd even driven through a couple nearby parks, because… huh, she really couldn't remember why. Only the gauge on her dashboard hovering over E forced her to stop.

In the mid-afternoon sun, she filled up her tank and pondered what to do. With the rest of the day. With her job. With her life. Status quo was unsustainable. If Frank told her he'd been joking or having a psychotic breakdown, she still wouldn't continue to work for Hilda. She'd been a fool for continuing there as long as she had.

Her phone still rested on the passenger side floor mat, where she'd tossed it this morning. It mocked her. But she'd be damned if she turned the thing back on.

Nothing her boss could say to her would justify that action.

She'd destroyed family businesses to feed Frank's greed. She'd squandered her own reputation to build his. She'd burned all professional bridges so she could continue to swim in the cesspool that was the Hilda Timbers corporate culture. She had no family by which to compare his treatment. So she'd associated continued employment with caring. His regular check-ins with concern. Her bonuses for love.

There had to be a job out there that didn't force her to live her life at the devastation of others. But where and what? Frank wouldn't write her a letter of recommendation. He might very well actively impair any job prospects she could scrounge up.

Who would be fool enough to hire her?

Who would be fool enough to love her?

An overwhelming sense of failure trickled through her veins after that disastrous second make-out session with Ulrik. She'd thrown herself at him—*uh-gehn*—in spite of pretending she wasn't exactly as pathetic as Charlotte Larson. Eydís should just go ahead and retrieve her phone to get the requisite unsolicited booty pic out of the way. Because there was no way he'd want to put up with her after she'd left him hard and dry. *Uh-gehn.*

She couldn't go back to work. She couldn't go back to Ulrik. What was her next likely self-ruining-and-pathetic step in this game of life? She couldn't think of a one.

Life had declared checkmate against her. Game over.

Nowhere to go, no family, no friends. Her car somehow drove her to the Drekison family house.

She rang the doorbell, prepared to slink away when they answered, icy stares directed at her for the shitty way she'd treated their son. No way would they want to see her, much less talk to her. She should have returned to her hotel room.

"Hey there, hon." Steph's warm voice sounded on the other side of the door. "Give me a sec. This damn door sticks because we never use it. Everyone knows to come to the back door."

With a loud, wrenching objection, the door swung open, and Steph greeted Eydís with the sunniest smile she'd ever seen. Then yanked her into the house and wrapped her in a bone-crushing hug. "As my girls would say, *we got ya, fam. Come spill the tea!*"

Steph ushered Eydís directly to the kitchen with a wide smile and a comforting arm around her shoulders.

"Oh for joy, I am so glad you're here." Fröja's melodic voice met her before the woman rounded a corner and grabbed Eydís's hands in hers. "Ulrik was worried about you. I'm very relieved you found your way here."

Ulrik was worried about her? That made no sense. Maybe he was worried he hadn't had the chance to mock her. After all, she'd thrown herself at him. Twice. In spite of declaring otherwise. And twice, their make-out sessions had been interrupted.

And was *make-out* even descriptive enough for the intense passion she'd felt when in his arms? Not that semantics mattered because he likely wouldn't want a three-peat.

Fröja maneuvered her to the cozy breakfast nook and sat her down. Thank goodness, because Eydís moved like a robot, her brain unable to process thoughts or actions. A mug of steaming coffee appeared in front of her and a plate of delicious-looking buttery pastries slid next to it.

"Girl talk is best with caffeine and sugar." Steph declared as she slid onto the nearest chair.

"Well, when it's too early for wine." Countered Fröja as she sat across the small table.

Eydís wrapped her hands around the mug of coffee and stared into its inky depths as if she could find truth or inspiration or basic words. She didn't deserve these women. Her heart withered and the tears she'd held at bay all day finally flowed down her cheeks. "You're both so wonderful, but you shouldn't be here. Or rather, I shouldn't be here. I'll go. Please let Ulrik know—"

"Sit, dear." Fröja's voice was gentle, but firm. "Enjoy your coffee and *skillingsboller*."

"But, you don't know who I am. You don't know what I've done." Eydís shook head, her voice thick with emotion, and her body heavy with the guilt of her life. "What I'm supposed to do."

"Yes, we do." Steph patted her arm. "David Peterson might be a dimwit, but he's Einstein compared to his grandson Chad, whose lips are looser than that tramp Margaret Holsten."

"Wrong set of lips, Steph." Fröja chided, laughter in her eyes as she sipped her coffee. She addressed Eydís. "We know what you were ordered to do. We also know you weren't successful. I imagine that has put you in a problematic position with your employer. Eydís, dear, you are far too talented for them. They will suck your soul dry and leave your barren bones on the side of the road without a backward glance."

"She's right. They suck." Steph spoke around a mouthful of cinnamon roll. Her eyes widened on a thought and she practically bounced in her seat. "You should come work for us!"

"Wait. Stop. This full-frontal intervention is... overwhelming." Eydís set her coffee down and wiped at her lingering tears, hoping her bitterness didn't bleed into her voice. "Newfound seduction duties aside, my job responsibilities are to undermine the competition so they go belly up and Hilda can buy them out for practically nothing. Are you telling me Drekison Logging and Construction has a job opening for that?"

Fröja shook her head. "No, but we will always have a spot for intelligent, hardworking, devoted employees. The sheer fact you've worked for Frank Hilda for as long as you have proves you have those qualities."

"Well, we might have questioned the intelligence part, if we hadn't already met you." Steph winked. How could these two women simultaneously tease and uproot her very soul?

"Or my lengthy employment proves I have no scruples." Eydís mumbled under her breath, then addressed both women. "I appreciate the job offer, but I signed a noncompete clause with Hilda. I can't work for another logging or construction company for two years. Even if I hadn't signed the noncompete, I doubt

Ulrik wants to work anywhere near me now that he knows I was supposed to seduce him. Your family has been so kind to me, but I'm a caustic personality and eventually wear on everyone. You don't want me around, trust me."

"You can tell yourself that, dear. But it's a lie." Fröja's voice was soft and motherly. Or at least, what Eydís imagined a loving, understanding mother might sound like. The fact the older woman used that tone of voice with her, who should be considered the enemy where the Drekison family was concerned, was irrational. Yet Fröja leaned closer, as if to punctuate her words. "You are a strong, capable woman with a good heart, and just because weaker people can't handle that does not mean you are *caustic*. You are a warrior, and deserve to surround yourself with the like."

"Eydís." Steph's firm yet affirming voice pulled her attention before she could deny Fröja's statement. "You are a dragon. Don't let the little people try and tell you otherwise."

Her heart dropped to her feet. "I'm n-not a dragon!" Panic made her body tremble although as her mind knew they used the term *dragon* metaphorically and not literally. Still, she couldn't accept that anyone would think of her that way. She was sooo *not* a dragon. "I-I'm just someone who grew up in the foster care system, Steph. It made me distrustful and prickly. That's all. It's also why I grate on everyone sooner or later. I'm a little too... undomesticated... for most."

Both older women scoffed. Fröja waved away Eydís's confession. "That's what the weak want you to think of yourself. When we learned of Chad Peterson's confession, Ulrik's first thought was your well-being. My son likes you, Eydís. We all do. And we Drekisons happen to be excellent judges of character."

She stood and walked to Eydís and squeezed her shoulders as if to reassure her. As if to let her know she had a supporter in her corner of the boxing ring.

Steph also patted Eydís's hand. "We got your back, hon. And find the exact wording for that non-com so we can figure out a work-around. If you want to leave Hilda, we'll help make it happen, regardless of where you go."

Fröja topped off the coffee mugs and sat back down with a dismissive wave of her hand. "And don't let that *mordersnegle,* Frank, worry you. We've defeated adversaries that would make him piss himself."

Eydís's jaw dropped. They knew. Knew what she'd been sent here to do—what she'd failed to do through her incompetence— and still wanted her around? They'd even called her a warrior.

A warrior who'd spent all afternoon feeling sorry for herself and doing nothing to solve her own problems. When had she ever allowed herself to wallow in self-pity like this? When had she ever allowed self-pity, period. She'd always carried the remnants of her past like a knight carries his lady's favor into battle, only it wasn't a sign of love or admiration but a means to say *fuck you* to that abandonment and negligence.

That was her past. But what about her present? She had a bunch of apologies to make. Most of them to Ulrik. She trembled with a mix of uncertainty and excitement at the prospect. If Fröja was right and he truly cared for her, hopefully he would accept her apologies. The possibility focused her energy. Gave her something to do that wasn't mindless roaming and general avoidance.

"Ulrik told me to call him." Eydís could barely catch her breath, like she'd run a marathon. But her heart hammered from something other than aerobic exercise. Purpose beat at her chest. And renewed excitement. "But I don't have his number. Would you know where I could find him?"

Fröja slanted her a smile like Eydís had passed a test of sorts. "He volunteers at the local animal shelter on Tuesday afternoons. But you can find him in the woods once dusk hits."

"Until then, have a *skillingsboller* and let's gossip." Steph pushed the plate of pastries her way, mischief and laughter sparkling in her eyes.

～

Ugh. Fröja had said Eydís could find Ulrik in the woods. But *where,* exactly, amidst the hundreds of acres the Drekisons owned, had not been offered and Eydís had neglected to ask in her haste to *go after her man* as Steph had phrased it. If she'd had GPS, an ATV, and broad daylight, she'd be hard-pressed to find a single person wandering the woods, no matter that he was a tall and possibly naked Viking god.

Without any of that, the task was impossible. So she hunted down his parked truck to wait for him, reminiscent of the other night. Fortunately, she found his truck at the same spot as before. Then she found his pile of clothes, because of course she did.

Maybe spurred by the confidence that came with renewed purpose, or maybe something more instinctive guided her. She didn't hesitate to grab her phone—still not powered up, which at this point was a purposeful *fuck off* to her boss—and head deep into the early evening woods in search of the second-born Drekison brother. Perhaps she could convince him her attraction was honest. Perhaps she could lay out a few confessions that would start the ball rolling on a new direction in her life. At the very least, she hoped he'd give her the opportunity to apologize.

She walked through the endless woods, her footsteps muffled on the leafy, mossy forest floor. Waning sunlight dappled her skin through the trees, but the clear sky and full moon lent enough illumination she wouldn't stumble and twist an ankle in the growing evening. The birds chittered high above and critters rustled among the branches and fallen limbs. A distant breeze toyed with leaves and needles. These woods were busy with life, yet held a peacefulness that seeped into her bones.

Ulrik had been right. Being among these trees calmed and

energized. And Eydís wasn't even naked to enjoy the full power of that benefit.

She'd walked about an hour, her gaze scanning the surrounding forest like a visual bloodhound, hoping to catch a glimpse of Ulrik, when she felt a faint hum. An electric sort of energy buzzed along her skin, causing the hair on her arms to raise. A quick glance proved there were no power lines running through this area to explain why the air was so charged. Was there a power grid in the ground? That made no sense. The steady, relentless growth of tree roots would destroy any such infrastructure.

She continued, and the hum stopped. A couple silent minutes passed, and it resumed, beginning low in volume and intensity, then growing until a tremor shook the forest floor like a seismic quake. Surely this area wasn't on an undocumented fault line.

The cycle of silence followed by growing energy continued. Too consistent to be an act of nature, but electrical power did not ebb and flow like this. As she walked in the direction her gut sensed was the source, she realized she heard the buzzing, but not in her ears. She felt the hum in her bones, which was disturbing.

Contemplating the strange phenomenon, she climbed over a thick fallen log and up the side of a small ravine. When she reached the top, she stopped in her tracks, her heart in her throat.

Up ahead was something wiggling, waving, in the air, along the ground. Like a used car lot tube man slowly wafting about. And shiny. Emerald green and… scaled?

Was this a sort of fever dream? Was she being punked? Her heart lodged in her throat, afraid to discover the truth of this vision, because that would mean she'd finally fallen into insanity. And yet, Eydís wasn't given to flights of fancy. Ever. But still, she doubted what she saw with her eyes just as soundly as her heart and her head screamed it could only be one thing.

A dragon tail.

Slowly, quietly, she approached. If she blinked away the hallucination, what horror could possibly stand in its place? Yet with each step forward, the illusion never wavered or disappeared. The closer she got, her initial reaction was confirmed. Which was more unnerving because there was no way this was an actual dragon. Her view of the casually flicking tail grew to include a serpentine body with short legs ending in blunt claws, and finally an elegantly long, practically canine-shaped head, jagged ridges along its jawline and a crest that resembled shards of wood. Its head, snout to skull, pressed against a tree, its eyes closed in concentration. The humming buzz she'd felt in her body was so powerful now, her teeth clattered and her lips and fingertips tingled.

The potent energy emanated from the beast. The dragon. An actual fucking dragon.

Eydís's legs buckled, and she crumpled to the soft ground. All her life, she'd thought dragons existed because she'd remembered from her early years that she should have one inside her. That she'd been denied her family because she lacked the one requirement to be loved. Had learned early in her foster years to keep that information to herself because it only ever got her in trouble or mocked. But maybe her five-year-old self had simply imagined the whole thing to explain why her family could give her up. Honestly, none of the dragon shifter books she'd furtively read as a teen ever fully explained how it was possible to shift from human form to dragon. Shifters were the creations of fiction and dragons were the creatures of myth.

Yet, here was a dragon straight from the pages of an artist's mind.

Hope and excitement burst through her body, and she carefully crept closer to the distracted creature. Was it sleeping? Was it truly the source of the buzzing in her veins?

She had to touch it. Had to experience the truth for herself. And if it ate her, or if this turned out to indeed be a hallucination and it was really a momma bear that mauled her to protect its cubs, so be it. Every atom of her being cried out to know beyond a doubt that this creature existed. That her miserable childhood and all her personal failings hadn't just been imagined or misplaced. As if, by proving to herself that dragons actually existed, being *NeiDreki* wouldn't be such a horrible fate to endure because it at least acknowledged the possibility of having a dragon within.

Driven by a need more powerful than logic and sanity and even her mottled feelings about discovering the truth, Eydís stood when she reached the tree, lifted her hand, and placed it on the beautiful, iridescent green scales of the dragon's cheek.

POW!

Energy lit her up, then all went dark.

CHAPTER THIRTEEN

W *hat. The. Hell?*
Ulrik blinked and glanced down at his naked body, his ears ringing as if from a bomb. He'd been in his dragon form a moment ago, channeling powers to eradicate the beetles and larvae from the infested tree and bolster its strength to recover, which he'd been doing most evenings for the past few weeks.

Then, a surge of power exploded through his dragon, yanking him into his human form, and the tree was… Gone. Just… gone, with only a shattered stump as evidence it had ever existed. Leaves and pine needles and splinters of wood rained down. Spots of his skin itched with sticky sap and the air was thick with the scent of pine. Had a grenade detonated? Was this a war zone? Was he under attack?

What in Odin's name had caused the tree to explode, leaving only the smallest fragments?

He glanced around the forest floor, which looked like someone had tossed around a half-assed mulch bed. The tiny beetles and larvae littered the ground, crisp as if electrocuted.

Then he saw the body.

Eydís lay about ten yards away, her body dirt- and leaf-covered and steaming as if from being near a fire. Or a bomb.

She wasn't breathing.

Heart in his throat, he raced to her, sliding to his knees despite the layer of splintered tree shrapnel. He checked her vitals. No breath. No heartbeat. He flattened his palms on her chest and pumped.

"Come on, *lítill fura*. You are too tough to let death claim you." He'd never been so frantic before, not even when battling *Níðhöggr*. "If you don't live, I'll tell Owen Carson you desired him."

Nothing. Ulrik lowered to give her mouth to mouth. Three puffs of breath in, and she came to, gasping and arching, her eyes popping open. Before he could pull back, she wrapped her arms around his neck and pulled him down for a desperate kiss he felt down to his toes.

She'd just gotten her breath back, and now took his away. Then she slipped her tongue into his mouth.

That, he felt down to his cock.

Unsure how a near-death experience could manifest as such intoxicating passion, but by the Allfather, he could no longer act the gentleman with her. His relief was too great and his desire too strong. He kissed her with all the longing in his heart. Their tongues danced, their lips hungry for purchase, both of them moaning and clutching at each other as if afraid the other might disappear. He gently pulled her more fully into his arms, his weight pinning her to the spongey bed of the forest detritus.

Eydís's fingernails dug into his back and she arched against him as he plundered her mouth. He laced his fingers through her hair, frizzled and tangled at the ends as if singed, and slanted his head for a better angle to thrust his tongue into her mouth, wishing it was his cock plunging into her heat.

She tore her mouth away from his and Ulrik paused, his body

trembling with the need to continue. Even burning with desire for this woman, he was aware enough to wait for her to allow it.

"Ulrik! How long was I out? Did you see it? Was it still here when you found me?" She gasped, searching his face with an expression of wonder that had nothing to do with his kisses. Still, a man could pretend. Her gaze raked his body, or at least what she could see from her prone position. "Why are you—wait, forget that, I'm not surprised you're naked."

Ulrik settled his body further between her legs and propped himself on his forearms. He was desperate to kiss her, and his erection, nestled at the apex of her thighs, concurred. But Eydís obviously wanted to talk. Kisses would have to wait. He brushed his fingertips along her jawline. "I don't know how long you were out, *lítill fura*. Hopefully only a few moments because you weren't breathing."

"Not breathing?" She didn't sound shocked or concerned, merely curious. "Huh, maybe it did try to kill me."

"What tried to kill you?" He couldn't be as cavalier as Eydís about her possible death, and instinctively tensed to battle whatever creature had attacked her, glancing around the growing evening light of the forest for the threat.

"Well, I'm still alive thanks to you, so it didn't succeed." She shook her head and traced her fingers along his shoulder tattoos. Huginn and Muninn, the raven pair from Norse mythology that flew around Midgard to bring news to Odin. They represented his role as second to the heir. A useless role these last several years.

Eydís looked at him, a shy smile on her lips. "Ulrik, I saw a dragon. A great, green dragon as wide as a tree trunk and long as a semi-truck. Did you see it when you got here? Did you see it when it left? I touched it. I couldn't stop myself, I had to touch it. Then a boom like a lightning bolt, and everything went black."

"You…" He struggled to gather his thoughts. For a human, Eydís was shockingly calm for having just seen and touched his dragon. In fact, she seemed more enchanted by the experience than terrified. "You saw a dragon and your first thought was to touch it?"

"If I'd seen a unicorn, my reaction would have been the same. So touch a mythological danger noodle? Hell yeah." She laughed. Then her expression sobered and she gripped his biceps. "Ulrik, I have a confession to make about why I was sent here. I think you already know what it is."

He merely nodded. She'd been sent to fuck over his family's business. By using him as a chump. While he believed Hilda Timbers would stoop to something so reprehensible, he couldn't convince himself Eydís would follow through. Maybe he was naive. Maybe she was his personal blind spot. But he was willing to take the risk, if it meant the chance to strip her of her emotional armor as readily as her clothes.

She bit her lip and frowned. "I've been an excellent Hilda Timbers employee over the years. I tried to warn you away a few times, if you remember. Not that you listened."

"Hearing only what I want happens to be one of my super powers." He gave her a half-smile and reached down to run his hand along her thigh and wrap it around his waist, thrusting once for emphasis. Her fingers flexed and she bit back a small moan. It took all his self-restraint to bring his attention back to their conversation and the point he wanted to make. "When we were together, did you fake any of it?"

"No!" Her eyes widened with surprise. Then she worried her bottom lip again. "I would understand if you don't believe me. Hilda Timber's North American Project Manager isn't really me. I thought it was. But apparently there's at least one line I won't cross."

Ulrik rolled their entwined bodies over and sat up so she straddled him, grimacing and readjusting when his butt cheek landed on a particularly pointy piece of tree shrapnel. "Eydís, you are a badass shield maiden and Hilda Timbers doesn't deserve you. It's your choice, but if you leave them, I will do whatever I can to help you find a job that makes you happy."

"That's pretty much what your mom and aunt said when I stopped by the house." She pulled his head down and brushed her lips across his. "Ulrik, I already quit my job. I submitted my official resignation to HR, including all the nasty emails and voicemails my boss sent me in his completely unhinged rage today. Nothing will happen to him, but it makes my resignation pretty nonnegotiable."

She smiled, her fingers threading through the hair at the base of his scalp. It both tickled and shot desire straight to his already-throbbing cock, pulling his attention away from their conversation. If she'd applied this tactic from the very beginning, he might very well have considered selling his family out. Ulrik cleared his throat. "Not to make you feel judged, but why did you stay with them for so many years?"

"Because apparently hearing only what I want to hear is my super power, too." She tried to joke, but her smiled faltered. Then her face fell. "I thought they appreciated me. I thought my contribution was meaningful. I thought... I thought they were the only ones willing and able to put up with my aggressive nature. Turns out, they were just using me."

"Eydís." He breathed her name as her tears streamed down her cheeks, and pulled her in for a tight hug. Damn him for asking the question that made her cry. "Discovering your ally is actually your enemy is a real kick to the guts. I'm sorry you had to experience that."

For several minutes, he held her and rubbed her back, giving her time to flow through the emotions of her personal discovery. Of her confession. As it ebbed, he smiled against her hair and made his own confession. "Want to know a secret? I'm not really sorry Hilda was such a horrible employer. Not if they're the reason you're in my arms right now."

"Sorry, not sorry, huh." Her laugh against his neck was soft and watery.

Finally, she sniffed and straightened. She flashed him a hopeful smile, but her eyes were shadowed with doubt. "Want to know my secret? I'm supposed to have a dragon in me."

Just as his family had suspected. She was a shifter. That made more sense than her being a mere human. But she'd said she was *supposed* to have a dragon. Meaning she didn't. Meaning she was *NeiDreki*. Was she the rumored one the New York clan had been given up?

Anger sliced through him on her behalf, and he flinched. She must have assumed it was shock, because she nodded. "It's true. But I don't. I was born without one, and my family didn't want me because of that. So I grew up in foster homes instead."

Rumor confirmed, but he hated the truth of it.

"So, your family abandoned you because you are *NeiDreki*?" Anger morphed into rage at her clan for turning their back on a child, just because it had not been born according to their expectations. Lucia had grown up with emotional abuse from her own parents because she hadn't met their expectations. What the fuck was wrong with his kind if they thought any of that was acceptable? "Eydís, the dragon chooses us. The child shouldn't be blamed if one does not."

"I agree, but for whatever reason—wait, you know what *NeiDreki* is? How do you know what *NeiDreki* is? Why aren't you freaking out?"

Ulrik moved her off his lap and stood, ignoring how her gaze flicked to his erection, and backed up several paces. He relaxed his hold on his inner beast. With the same desperate need and enthusiasm as when his dogs rush outside for the first morning piss, his dragon burst forth for Eydís to see exactly why he could possibly know about *NeiDreki*.

He watched her reaction through the sharp focus of a predator's eyes, relieved she wasn't the least bit afraid. Shock and awe immediately gave way to delight. She gasped and sighed, a dazzling smile on her face. Birthdays and Christmas and the defeat of *Níðhöggr* all rolled into one moment couldn't match the elation in her expression. Her gaze drank him in.

And damn if his dragon didn't preen under the adulation.

"Woooooow." Her voice was soft, her tone enthralled, and her eyes wide and shimmery like Japanese anime. "Ulrik, is that really you?"

He made the dragon nod. When he shifted back, he could better explain the nuanced relationship between man and beast. For now, it was close enough to the truth.

She approached, slowly, as if he might either attack or run away. His dragon chittered in laughter. She hiked a brow at him. "Are you laughing at me?" When he nodded, she crossed her arms and shifted her weight to a hip. "Not all of us get to see mythical creatures every day. I'm trying to make the most of it."

Fearless, like a true shield maiden.

His dragon laid down, his long body threaded around the surrounding tree trunks to be as patient and unthreatening as possible, not that Eydís was afraid of him. After she got her visual fill, she approached his head, her hand lifted to touch him again.

When her soft, small hand made contact, an electric current rippled over his scales, like touching an exposed plug. They both shivered. Had she felt the jolt as well? Her eyes enamored with every inch of his dragon—dammit, now Ulrik was jealous of his own internal beast—she ran her hands along its neck and sides. The dragon's power fluttered beneath his scales, a racehorse straining to be given free rein to run. Her every touch electrified, energized. Intensified. He'd never felt this formidable before.

On an inspired thought, he reached his power out to the nearest tree, as cautiously as reaching for a fragile crystal wine glass. Energy from her touch followed, amplifying his power.

Using only a fraction of the normal level, he cleared the tree of beetles and larvae in just a minute.

And Eydís had no idea she'd helped.

She glanced briefly at the tree that still shook from their cleansing. But her concentration was on the dragon. Touching him, staring at him, leaning in to smell him. As if she was memorizing him; as if she was convincing herself he was real. His dragon leaned his head to her, butting his muzzle against her body. She rightfully assumed he wanted a hug, and wrapped her arms around his face, leaning her own cheek against his forehead.

His dragon pooled his power, circled it around the emptiness that should host a dragon, picking up speed and force with each cycle like a particle collider, then sent it radiating outward as a shockwave, pulsing against a dozen trees simultaneously. Barely thirty seconds later, the trees had expunged their dead beetles and the upper branches trembled with the life-affirming power coursing through them.

A shower of leaves and needles finally jerked Eydís's attention away from the dragon. She looked around, blinking like she'd awaken from a trance. "What just happened?"

The dragon faced her, and Ulrik regarded her through the beast's eyes. He answered her via the mental communication. "You *happened, Eydís.*"

"*I* happened?" Her face screwed up in confusion. "I must be having a psychotic breakdown because I'm petting a dragon and you're talking in my head. But I'm just gonna go with it because it's about the least weird thing I've dealt with today."

"*You're not having a breakdown.*"

"Says the voice in my head. Look, you sound all impressed with me, but I'm not the one who can turn into a dragon. I told you, I'm—"

"*NeiDreki, yes. You were born without a dragon, but you were still born with the space for one. That hollow area way down deep inside where a dragon was meant to reside within you.*" His dragon tapped its muzzle against the center of her chest, even though the space Ulrik spoke of wasn't a physical place in the body. It was far more abstract, but just as real.

She rubbed the area and frowned. "" I-I always assumed this empty feeling was because I'd been abandoned by my family."

"*Does it go away when you're with us?*"

"No. But it no longer hurts." She shook her head. "It's just... there. Why does being with you and your family make such a difference?"

His dragon did his best to shrug. This conversation would be so much easier if Ulrik shifted back. But honestly, a man could only take so much and if he pulled Eydís into his arms yet again to comfort her, his version of *comfort* might be unwelcome. Especially for a woman still working through the truth of her heritage. Who had recently quit her job after being ordered to seduce him.

The dragon wrapped its tail around her in its own semblance of an embrace. She smiled and rubbed her cheek against his slick scales.

"*Maybe the ache of that space eases when you're with your own kind. I know this explanation won't erase the pain of abandonment you've endured, but Father says sending* NeiDreki *to live with humans is a long-standing practice.*" Did Uncle Bodil's children suffer the emptiness Eydís did? They were also *NeiDreki*, so it was possible, though they'd never mentioned it. But their mother was human. Maybe that was the difference. However, that was a conversation for another day. Ulrik refocused on the beautiful woman currently sneaking a peek beneath his dragon's lips to the fangs beneath.

"*Eydís, your empty space... I think it acts like an amplifier for power. When my dragon swung his power through your hollow space, your emptiness magnified it a thousand-fold. We accomplished in less than a minute what would have taken an hour alone."*

"What are you—" She stared at the beetle bodies littering the ground around them. "Are you exterminating the beetles from the trees?"

"My dragon's power is wood. I've been infusing the trees with a frequency of power that kills the beetles and their larvae, and then boosting the tree's strength against future beetles."

"And being with me… helped?"

The hope in her voice nearly did him in. Her boss had gutted her pride recently. He'd reduced her from successful businesswoman to little more than a tool. A meaningless stepping stone for him to achieve his goals. So shortsighted on his part because Eydís was much more than a means to an end. She was powerful. Intelligent. Loyal.

Sexy.

His dragon stretched out low and jerked his head toward his back. *"Yes, you helped. Hop on board and I'll show you just how much."*

CHAPTER FOURTEEN

E ydís was riding a dragon. A real fucking dragon. A dragon that was also a sexy-as-hell Ulrik. She had obviously died, because this was too much of a dream-she'd-never-known-she'd-had come true.

And she was okay with that. In fact, she was better than okay.

Quitting Hilda had lifted a crushing weight of self-hate she hadn't realized she'd carried. She'd cleansed her life of a massive toxic relationship, and damn if she wasn't lighter and more hopeful and joyous than she could ever remember.

Or maybe that was because she was riding a mythological beast through a forest and, together, they were ridding trees of a murderous invasion like some crime-fighting dynamic duo. And maybe because she knew the dragon would eventually shift back into a very naked Viking god with whom she wanted to finish all the false starts they'd endured these past few days. He'd been hard as a rock against her hip during their confession conversation. And yet he'd been gentleman enough not to push anything sexual because she'd needed his emotional support. And he somehow knew that.

All these years, she'd assumed only Hilda Timbers had understood and supported her feral personality.

Then she'd met the Drekison family. She'd met Ulrik. They supported her. Encouraged her. Accepted her.

Loved her.

Turns out she wasn't actually feral. Not as much as she'd felt all those years working for Frank. She'd traveled a rough road to get here, and she probably needed a therapist to work through her childhood trauma. But she was stronger as a result. A shield maiden, as Ulrik and his family called her.

The truth of this was a shocking revelation she never would have made if she hadn't met the Drekisons.

And, most shocking of all, her status as *NeiDreki* wasn't the scarlet letter she'd always thought it was. In fact, it was a power unique to her. Rather than lament her lack of a dragon, even though it would be totally awesome to shift into one herself, she carried her status with pride. Within a couple hours, she and Ulrik had rid half the infested trees of beetles.

If she hadn't met the Drekisons, she never would have learned any of this.

If they hadn't met her, Ulrik would still be battling beetles one tree at a time.

She sent a mental *thank you* to Frank for being an utterly greedy, unscrupulous asshat. Else she wouldn't at this moment be astride a gorgeous green serpentine dragon, saving the world and anxiously awaiting the moment she could wrap her legs around Ulrik's torso instead.

"Lítill fura, *you keep thinking those thoughts, and I won't last long enough to pleasure you.*" Ulrik groaned in her head.

"Are you reading my mind?" The possibility was both unsettling and comforting.

"*Not your exact thoughts. But I seem to be very in tune with your feelings. Like at dinner last night. And at the office this morning. And, honestly, if you don't stop thinking about sex, I'm going to blow before our next kiss."*

She laughed. She had never before felt so light and carefree. "Then I guess you'll just have to rally for a second attempt because I want you in my mouth."

The dragon dropped to the ground and she squealed from the rapid descent. This was better than any theme park thrill ride. As they hit the mossy ground, Ulrik shifted, rolled her onto her back, and pinned her with his weight. He smiled at her, his eyes glittering with laughter and lust. "Before you put anything in your mouth, *lítill fura*, these damn clothes are coming off."

He worked the buttons and zippers of her business suit with swift efficiency, trailing kisses as her skin was revealed. Soon enough, Eydís was as naked as Ulrik, the cast-off clothing and the soft mossy grass of the small clearing a comfortable mattress beneath them, the full moon through the few branches their illumination. The late August evening was warm with just enough nip in the night air to punctuate the heat of arousal in her body.

Ulrik sat back on his heels and gazed at her. Eydís had never been self-conscious about her curves, but she'd also never known such intense worship as what she saw in his eyes. His gaze was a caress. He spread her knees wide, opening her core for his perusal, and licked his lips as if before a banquet. She squirmed under his gaze, arousal trickling through her folds. "Eydís, you are so beautiful, fully clothed or naked. Not sure why I waited until now to tell you."

"In your defense, I was a bit of a bitch. That doesn't invite compliments." She lifted her leg and traced a toe along the ladder of his obliques. He sucked in a breath when she hit a ticklish spot. "Besides, fully clothed beauty doesn't always equal naked beauty. I might have had scales instead of skin."

He chuckled and shot her a smirk. "I'm a dragon shifter. Scales would be totally sexy, too."

He covered her body with his, but she pressed a hand against his chest before he could do anything. Understanding dawned and he rolled to his back, carrying her over as he did. She straddled his torso, loving the view. Holy shit Ulrik was hot. Stacks of muscles rippled whenever he moved. He folded his arms behind his head, his biceps flexing deliciously. This morning at the office, those arms had lifted her like she was a feather. Her curves could be as intimidating as her personality, but Ulrik had taken it all with the same serenity as the forest. He was as solid and patient as an oak tree.

Speaking of solid oak—

Ulrik adjusted his position beneath her, and it thrust her up like a bucking bronco. She laughed and braced her hands on his rock-hard abs for support. Speaking of rock hard, his erection was an ever-present entity at her back. She wanted it front and center.

Before he could move or stop her, she shimmied down his tree trunk thighs and settled between them, loving the view of the lone log at their apex. Thick and already seeping pre-cum, so long there was no way she could take all of it in her mouth. But she salivated for the opportunity to try. She grasped his cock around the base, her fingers barely touching, and Ulrik hissed a moan. Then she pumped a few times, loving its silky skin and the firmness underneath, and licked the path of the vein that ran the course from testicles to bulbous head.

She would gladly continue her exploration of his taste and texture, but she'd been enough of a dick-tease already since meeting Ulrik. And she was desperate to fill her mouth. So she did, taking him to the back of her throat in one smooth downward stroke that forced a shocked gasp out of him. Eydís bobbed and sucked and swirled her tongue around the sensitive hood, flicking and licking at the tasty pre-cum flowing from the tip. Was it a shifter thing, to be so addicting? Desperation flowed through her veins, she wanted him to come in her mouth, down her throat, fill her with his salty essence more than she wanted professional affirmation and her next breath—

"You're going to kill me, *lítill fura*." Ulrik's strong hands pulled her off as he growled. "My turn to have some fun."

"That wasn't fun for you?" She giggled as he grabbed her thighs and lifted her to his chest like lifting a plate of *skillingsboller*.

"That was amazing and I hope you want to do that again. Soon." He grunted, pulling her slick core to his mouth. "But right now, I want you to fuck my face."

His strong arms banded her thighs as she rode his mouth and tongue, his beard whiskers tickling the sensitive flesh of her inner thighs. He licked her length, covering his face in her juices and moaning in ecstasy with each swipe. He nibbled on her folds, sucked on her clit, devoured her until all she could do was close her eyes and enjoy the ride. She leaned into his hands as they worked magic on her breasts, squeezing and plucking her nipples, while his mouth did the same to her clit. Her thighs trembled as her orgasm hit her and she screamed her release to the stoic trees and the quiet night.

Then she was on her back, Ulrik's forearm cushioning her head and his other hand plumping and caressing her breasts while he kissed his way up her torso and neck. His solid thigh brushed against her sensitized clit, and her arousal blossomed again before it could fully retreat.

She needed him balls-deep inside her. Now.

"Eydís, I'm clean." He managed before he kissed her, thrusting his tongue into her mouth exactly the way she wanted him thrusting his cock inside her. He came up for air, to reposition his lips on hers and rush out another sentence. "But I don't have a condom."

She wrapped her arms around him, clutching for purchase on his sweat-slick skin, as desperate as he to finally consummate their passion for one another. "I'm clean, too." She sucked on his tongue like she'd sucked on his cock and the log against her thigh grew even harder, if that was possible. "And I'm on the pill."

On an agonized moan, he spread her legs with his knees and notched his cock at her entrance. Then pulled back just enough to look her in the eyes. She saw his need, his desperation, but also saw his self-control. Felt it in his labored breaths and the flex of his muscles to keep from thrusting. "Eydís. Beautiful. Tell me no or tell me you want to drive this train. Otherwise I'm not stopping until you scream again."

She wrapped her legs around his waist and squeezed, pulling until his cock was buried inside her, filling her, and they both moaned at the rightness of it.

"Promise you'll make me scream again?" She threaded her fingers through his hair and smiled.

Ulrik groaned again as he kissed her and moved his hips, thrusting long and deep with a roll at the end that took her breath away. "Yes, or I'll die trying."

With that vow, he wrapped his hands around her shoulders and set a blistering pace. His hips pistoned and his hands grounded her so she didn't fly forward with each thrust. Her pebbled nipples rubbed against his chest and he kissed the air from her lungs. Their moans combined and rose in volume. Her body bloomed, and her legs slid to the side as she grew helpless to do anything but feel. The rising tide of her pleasure, her release, barreled down to drown her in amazing sensations.

"Do you feel that, Ulrik?" She panted. He'd said he could sense her emotions. Could he sense her physical release? "Do you sense my orgasm?"

"Fuuuuuck yes." He growled against her neck. "Christ on a cracker, Eydís, it's amazing. You're amazing."

Her release detonated across her body and she screamed just like he'd promised. He followed and they both cried out to the silent audience of trees and moonlight, their bodies shuddering in spasms as they slowly floated down from that glittering height.

"No offense to your dragon, but *that* was better than any theme park thrill ride." She muttered against his cheek, the weight of his body sinking her into the soft moss mattress.

Ulrik chuckled, then rolled them to the side and wrapped her in the warmth of his embrace. Eydís was boneless, breathless, more replete and at peace than she could ever remember being. Was it just a wonderful side effect of amazing sex, or was it the man as well? And why was she contemplating such deep questions when all she wanted to do was sleep?

"You know, we could go to my cabin and do this again. On a proper bed." Lips brushed her forehead, and Ulrik's voice lulled her further. "Or we could just sleep. Hell, we could argue, if you want. As long as you're in my arms, I don't care what we do."

"I'll have to put my clothes back on." He made an unhappy noise at that, but stroked her back and thigh as she nestled further into his embrace. "While the thought of sleeping in each other's arms beneath the stars sounds romantic enough, I think I'd prefer to be in a proper bed. Besides, I have a job search to begin once the sun's up."

Ulrik made a yummy noise. "I have a position you could fill."

"Just one?" Eydís giggled. Giggled! When had she ever felt relaxed and happy enough to giggle?

"Well, one position at a time." He murmured. "But the possibilities are endless." He pulled back on a thought. "Just, no whips and chains, please."

She giggled again. "Okay. No whips and chains. For now."

CHAPTER FIFTEEN

"You both know how happy this makes me." Mother smiled as she filled their coffee cups.

After a mental conversation with the entire family this morning to bring everyone current on the success Ulrik had achieved eradicating beetles thanks to the crucial part Eydís played, they had checked her out of her hotel, returned her rental car, grabbed a box of Emerson's Bakery crullers, and headed to the family home to get Mother's help in brainstorming job possibilities for Eydís.

The twinkle in Mother's eyes confirmed her comment wasn't about any job.

"Not sure what you mean, Mother." Ulrik played dumb, but the fact Eydís practically sat in his lap at the breakfast table, and they couldn't keep their hands off each other, was pretty blatant evidence of their budding relationship.

Dare he say, of their blooming love.

Maybe he was merely a fleeting affair for Eydís. It was a distinct possibility, but he sensed a deeper connection with her. And his feelings for her certainly were more of a permanent nature.

"This makes me happy, too." Eydís palmed his cheek and sighed like a cat with a belly full of cream. "He makes me a better person."

Ulrik kissed her, the chaste brush of his lips on hers a promise of more decadent kisses later on in the privacy of his cabin. Well, as private as they could get with his five tongue-lolling rescue dogs jostling for attention.

Like every stray he'd ever brought home, Eydís had fit right in.

Mother nodded in that sage way of hers. "He does that for all of us, dear. He takes what's broken in us and makes us whole."

Eydís gazed in his eyes, her own burning with love. "Yes. It's his superpower."

Ulrik couldn't deny himself another, far less chaste, taste of her lips.

"So the rumors are true." Father's voice at the back door made Ulrik flinch. He was normally too aware of his surroundings for someone to sneak up on him. Then again, he normally wasn't distracted by the kisses of the woman he loved.

Loved. His heart stumbled at the truth. He loved Eydís. Hopefully one day she could return the emotion.

He cleared his throat. "Father, what are you doing here?"

"Thought I might get a little afternoon delight." He grabbed a coffee mug and kissed his wife's forehead before settling at the table beside her.

Ulrik made a gagging noise. "Not what I wanted to hear."

"Don't ask if you don't want the answer." Father chuckled. He sipped his coffee, then speared Ulrik and Eydís with a meaningful look. "Chad Peterson is losing his shit because a certain *former* Hilda Timbers employee is not playing her part in the destruction of Drekison Logging."

Eydís shrugged. "They can't blame me for going off-script when they never asked my consent to play that part to begin with."

"Is Eydís at risk of being attacked?" Ulrik tensed, pulling her closer against his body. He'd battled *Níðhöggr* to save his world, his family. He'd battle worse to save the woman he loved.

"I can't anticipate what Frank Hilda will do. And we should probably prepare for the worst." Father shook his head. "But Chad won't do a thing. Enough of us know about his part behind all this that the Petersons can't sweep it under the rug. And David has no doubt already yanked that pup's ear and explained in no uncertain terms how his actions reflect poorly on the family name."

A thought wrenched Ulrik's heart. "Do my actions reflect poorly on our family name?"

Was this perhaps why Father and Arkyn had distanced the company's daily business from Ulrik's influence over the years?

Three pairs of eyes regarded him with utter confusion. Father spoke first. "What do you mean by that, son?"

Ulrik shrugged, struggling to put his thoughts into actual words. "I've fallen in love with a competitor's employee. *Former* employee. I was the weak link she found that could possibly undo our family—"

"Listen here, *Baby Girl*." Eydís called him the name from their first meeting. "First of all, I am a badass shield maiden; I don't do weak links. So if you're wondering why I chose you over the first born son, rest assured it's because you are worthy enough for me." She punctuated that declaration with a loud pop of a kiss.

He brushed her hair behind her ears. "I don't mean that *you* actually deceived me. I am too attuned to your feelings to think that, *lítill fura*. I speak only of my own failings compared to my brothers."

"Eydís is right. You're no weak link, *drengr*." Mother snorted. "Neither are you a failure."

"You say that, Mother, but you also said I have an open heart.

That makes me vulnerable. Too easily deceived by swindlers. A sucker for lost causes and homeless dogs."

"I don't remember you ever being deceived, swindled, or suckered." Father shook his head. "You'd have a lot more dogs if that were the case."

"Ulrik, I said you have an open heart." Mother crossed her arms and hiked an eyebrow at him as if he'd completely misunderstood her. "I also told you that was not a weakness. It's a blessing for our family."

"Your mother is right, Ulrik." Father reached across the table and rested a comforting hand on his shoulder. "Arkyn might be the heir, with the strength to lead this clan and our company. But you are our heart."

"I know, I'm the second-born. The backup." Ulrik nodded and refrained from rolling his eyes. This wasn't news to him.

"That's not what I said." Father frowned at him like he should know better. "You are the heart. The glue that binds this family. Without you, we would be brittle shells of ourselves."

His parents normally offered sage wisdom, but this crap sounded like something from a woo-woo self-help book. Or one of Lin's fortune cookies. "If I'm so important, then why do you and Arkyn discuss the business and make decisions without my input? Why am I just a fly on the wall in meetings? The heir's silent spare? You do just fine without me."

Father's face screwed up in confusion, as did Mother's. Father shook his head as if to clear it. "Ask for your input? When do my sons sit back and allow life to happen to them?"

"I don't allow—" Ulrik wanted to yell, but the truth of Father's words shut his mouth. Growing up, he and Arkyn had been close as twins, their thoughts aligning more often than not. Even so, Ulrik had never hesitated to say his piece. None of the Drekisons did. When had he let his voice go silent?

His opinions had so often mirrored Arkyn's and Father's,

he'd stopped wasting the effort to verbally agree. And at some point, that silence had morphed into a muteness he'd misconstrued as indifference from his family. He deflated against the back of his chair. "Well, *Sorðinn.* Have I just been feeling sorry for myself all this time?"

The expressions on his parents' faces confirmed that truth.

He scrubbed his face in frustration. "I'm an asshole, aren't I?"

"Don't let Ivar hear you say that, dear." Mother chuckled. "He'll be upset to think he has competition for that title."

Father smiled and sipped his coffee.

Eydís sighed as if exhaling a lifetime of woe. "Don't beat yourself up too hard for misunderstanding your own truth. You're in good company for that."

He hugged her, resting his chin atop her head. "*Lítill fura,* do not believe for a moment that I have the same right as you to question my place in this world. In this family."

He pulled back to gaze in her eyes so she could see his sincerity. "And I hope you never question your place in *this* family."

"I guess that depends on one thing." She met his gaze with a sincerity of her own. "Let's readdress one of your earlier comments. Do you really love me?"

The battle between hope and doubt in her voice nearly did him in. He brushed his fingertips across her cheek. "I love you more than Ivar loves Jell-O salad. Give me time to prove it to you."

"Only if you also give me time to prove I love you." Her inhale trembled with emotion and tears shimmered in her eyes. "Ulrik Drekison, I love you. Will you marry me?"

Mother squealed with glee, Father hummed with satisfaction, and Ulrik smiled with all the joy bursting in his heart. His feisty, prickly *NeiDreki* love would forever surprise and delight him.

"As much as it would pain Charlotte Larson, I would be honored to be your husband, *lítill fura.*"

Eydís pressed her forehead to his and released a breath like she'd been holding it her entire life. "That's the right answer, *Baby Girl.*"

EPILOGUE

"It's your call, Eydís. But I think the New York clan should be included." Jólnir stood across the war room table from her as if they were discussing important Drekison Logging and Construction business.

In truth, they were talking about her wedding plans.

"I agree with Father." Arkyn piped in, not that she'd asked for his opinion on the matter. And not that he required her permission to express it. None of the Drekison family members, even Bodil and Steph's *NeiDreki* children, were shy with their opinions.

Only Ulrik kept quiet. He usually agreed with one of the other, vocal, family members— Eydís, most often—and felt no need to reiterate a point just to be heard. To speak or not to speak, it was his choice, and no one thought less of him for it. And neither did he.

The look he slanted her was a thumbs-up to speak for the both of them. She smiled at her future father-in-law, noting how joy flooded her heart like it did each time she was reminded she was now part of a family. And what a family it was. She couldn't have asked for a more supportive, loving, understanding, and wholesome one if she'd been given carte blanche at a build-your-own-family store. "Thank you. I will take the suggestion under advisement, Jólnir."

Ulrik hid his smile behind a hand. Arkyn snorted. "Father, that's big-corporate speak for *mind your own damn business,* dontcha know."

"Actually, in this case, it means *let's focus on Ty and Lin's wedding first.*" Ulrik countered. "They were the first to get engaged and Eydís and I have only been together a month. We have plenty of time to work through the logistics."

Jólnir laughed and lifted his hands as if in defeat. "All I know is someone better be making us grandbabies soon or your mother is going to implode."

"Will ya look at that?" Arkyn straightened and whipped his phone out as if receiving an important call. "I can't help ya with that request, Father."

The front doors burst open and in walked Bodil and Ivar, who took one look around and loudly declared to his father. "Geez Louise, can we get the weddings behind us before all this pressure to procreate?"

"The Dragon Council will expect you to be officially introduced so they can give their stamp of approval." Bodil addressed Eydís as if relaying bad news. The Drekisons didn't often speak about the Council, from which their clan and the New York clan had originated, but when they did, it was rarely complimentary. Eydís didn't know whether to be worried or annoyed that she might have to travel to Norway and be presented to the self-important council of dragon shifters who had historically washed their hands of *NeiDreki* as readily as her own parents had.

Ivar's smile was practically evil as he leaned toward her as if to share a secret. His voice carried through the room. "I might know someone with direct connects to the Council if you want to tell them to go fuck themselves."

He winked at her and she couldn't stop the giggle that bubbled up her throat. Lucia had shared her own story of growing up a complete disappointment to her Dragon Council parents, until recently when her dragon's amazing abilities had fully manifested, thanks to Ivar's support and encouragement. So, he could snub his nose at the Council all he wanted, but his future in-laws were members and he was trying to help pave the way for Lucia to rebuild her broken relationship with them.

Ivar might pride himself on being the resident asshole, but he was secretly a cinnamon roll.

"What the hell is this?" A loud, booming voice echoed from the front doorway.

Eydís cringed. Frank Hilda had been mysteriously quiet since she'd quit, perhaps because she'd tossed her company phone into the fire one evening at Ulrik's. But they knew he wouldn't go down with any amount of dignity.

"Hello, Frank." She waved to the other men in the room and made introductions. "These gentlemen are the heart and soul of Drekison Logging and Construction. You know, the company you tried to sabotage."

"You mean that *you* tried to sabotage." Frank sauntered into the room as if he had the right to stand next to these men. He glared at Eydís before kinda-not-quite glaring at the other men. "I had to come here myself and apologize to you in person for the reprehensible actions of my employee. Miss Helvig acted without my authority or approval, and her behavior flies in the face of cooperation and industry support that Hilda Timbers represents."

A long pause rang in the office, then the Drekison men burst into laughter so robust Ivar leaned against a desk and Arkyn held his side. Only Ulrik did not laugh. Instead, he turned to her to hide the green scales shimmering across his face and forearms. She sensed his fury as if it were her own, yet even she had never burned with such volatile anger at her former boss.

Frank Hilda didn't deserve that much emotional or physical energy.

She palmed Ulrik's cheek and planted a soft kiss on his lips to soothe him. He exhaled, forcibly calming his riotous emotions, then smiled at her before turning to face Frank again.

Frank's face was raw meat red and his sausage fingers fisted at his side. Eydís nearly laughed at his impotent rage. There was nothing he could do to any of them except verbally intimidate them. And the men in this room had battled a prophesized world-destroying entity the size of a continent. They would wipe the floor with Frank.

He pointed one of those sausage fingers at her. "You signed a noncompete clause. You can't work for them!"

Had she imagined the spittle flying from his mouth?

"I don't work for them, Frank. I am independently employed as a business consultant."

Meaning, she was getting paid to go out into the woods after hours with Ulrik and work their combined magic on the beetle infestation. It was a good gig, until the terms of her noncompete were over and they could hire her officially.

"Eydís, may I have your permission to utilize your amplifier?" Jólnir asked. Her hollow space could boost any of their powers, making her a weapon just as powerful as their dragons. Ulrik was training with her to close off access so no one could hijack her, and all the Drekisons were steadfast in asking her permission.

As if she could say no to any of these people she'd grown to love in such a short time.

She nodded. While she could hear their mental communications, she was as yet unable to respond in kind.

Power drifted through her. Eydís had become attuned to the subtle differences of each dragon. Jólnir's was a cool flow like a large river or underwater current. It whirled around her space a few times, gaining strength, then shot out in a pointed stream toward Frank.

His cunning expression turned vacant. Jólnir spoke softly, but his words carried a mass of power. "She is not the former employee you're looking for. You will return to your company and never seek her out again. And you will undo all the damage you have caused in your career."

"She's not the... I'll undo all the..." Frank muttered to himself as he turned and left the office as if in a trance.

Arkyn snorted. "Rude. He didn't even say good-bye."

"You're supposed to wave your hand when you go all Obi-Wan on us." Bodil snickered, demonstrating with a subtle rotation of his wrist.

"The Force is strong with you." Ivar teased.

Ignoring the others, Ulrik pulled Eydís within the circle of his arms, exactly where she wanted to be for the rest of her life. "*That's* your old boss? You could have taken him without Father's influence."

"True. But I don't have to do it all by myself anymore. Because you're my family now."

"I love the sound of that." He kissed her before she could agree.

ABOUT THE AUTHOR

Ava Cuvay is an award-winning bestselling author of out of this world Sci-fi and Paranormal Romance featuring sassy heroines, gutsy heroes, passion, adventure… and the word "moist".

She resides in central Indiana with her own scruffy-looking nerfherder and teen kiddos who think her "Rizz" is "cringe" but she "passes the vibe check" and her books "hit different." No cap.

She believes life is too short to bother with negative people, everything is better with Champagne, and Han Solo shot first. When not writing, Ava is thinking about writing. Or wine. And she's always thinking about bacon.

SIGN UP FOR AN EXCLUSIVE BONUS SCENE AND MORE BOOK NEWS!

Join my newsletter for exclusive bonus material, freebies, Advanced Reader Copy opportunities, and fun info! https://drinkingthestarspressllc.eo.page/2r3z6

STALK ME!

Check me out and follow me on your preferred platform:
Website for a complete listing of her books: AvaCuvay.com
Facebook Page: AvaCuvayAuthor
Goodreads Page: https://www.goodreads.com/author/show/15051407.Ava_Cuvay
BookBub: https://www.bookbub.com/authors/ava-cuvay

Amazon Author Page: https://www.amazon.com/Ava-Cuvay/
e/B01E5OIZ0I/

PLEASE LEAVE A REVIEW!

Book reviews are one of the few ways we authors receive
feedback from our readers. And we hunger for it! Please take a
few minutes and leave a review this book. Thank you!

"WHAT A DRAGON LOVES" SNEEK PEAK

ARKYN'S STORY

Arkyn Drekison is the alpha-heir of his Minnesota family's dragon shifter clan. Always at the front, in the know, and ahead of the curve. But his younger brothers have all found love and, for the first time in his life, he's... left behind. He can't fall for just anyone. He needs a dependable, feisty, steadfast shield maiden to love: a fellow shifter who can help lead his clan and mesh with the many strong personalities within his family. So why is he utterly captivated by a woman who is anything but? She's human, delicate, spacey, and far more comfortable with babies and pets than anyone old enough to make conversation. Yet there's something about her that entices his dragon and makes his earth power rumble with desire.
Amalthea Payne is a chaotic hot mess on a good day, always saying the wrong thing, easily distracted, and, well... just plain weird. She's unintentionally high-maintenance, and no one— friends and lovers, alike—needs the kind of bizarre she brings to the table. So she's a loner, which is probably for the best, because the mayhem churning deep in her soul is growing

stronger, threatening to suck her into a void of her own insanity.
Yet when she helps the tall, blonde, and gorgeous flannel-wearing-Thor-wannabee rescue a kitten, there's something about him that soothes her savage beast. Metaphorically speaking, of course.

Amalthea Celeste Payne, you need to quit goofing around and get your life together.

Her mother's terse words of wisdom—complete with the invocation of her full name to convey the gravity of it all—from yesterday's phone call still swirled around Ama's gut.

A full rotation of the Earth hadn't dulled the edge of those words, so often uttered over the years, and so often followed with a firm *You should be more like your sister.* Even a Saturday night spent at her favorite Minneapolis dance club, relinquishing her mind and body to the throbbing, incessant beat of her favorite Grindcore tunes, hadn't eased the pang of knowing she continued to disappoint. And now, driving home along the serene back roads of Minnesota, her favorite Shamanic EDM Spotify list blaring, she couldn't rid herself of the reality that—

Holy Frijoles, there's a dead man on the road!

Ama screeched to a halt behind a red pickup truck, hazards flashing, driver door open, and driver or someone else belly down on the asphalt, partially underneath the truck. Had he fallen out? Had the truck run him over?

Why did his ass look so good in those jeans?

She stared at the odd roadkill. Appreciating the view, yet sad such a nice ass had passed away. Then the body the ass was attached to lurched forward, further under the truck.

Ama screamed and jumped out of her car. Then leaned in to flick on the hazards. Then ran back to turn off the running engine.

"Are you injured? Should I dial 9-1-1? Why do we even use the word *dial* these days? Do you have any next of kin I should call?" She yelled as she ran to the side of the truck where the ass and two long legs still lay on the late-Spring-sun-warmed road. She kneeled beside them, twisting to look beneath the truck.

A voice hit her ears. A little muffled from the truck's running engine and a little strained. "I'm fine. Not injured. Just trying to get this kitten who ran out in front of me then ducked under my truck, dontcha know."

"Ooooh! Lucky duck, getting chosen by the cat distribution system." Ama flattened herself on the pavement to get a better view of the kitten. Two golden eyes stared at her from the shadows. It was... "Aww! You're a black cat! Hello there, handsome!"

"Hello there, back at ya." Both kitten and man turned to look at her. It was too dark to see which one spoke to her, but the voice was too deep to belong to the kitten, and it held a note of humor. "Are you a witch? Is this your familiar?"

"I think you mean Professor of the Dark Arts." She laughed and waved away his comment. "And, no. This is just my Saturday night clubbing makeup."

"An interesting look for Sunday morning. Did the club just let out?"

"*Pfffsh*. Minneapolis rolls its sidewalks up at 2am. I took a nap at a truck stop."

Wow, that was like four or five whole sentences spoken to a human being. That had to be a record for her. She usually clammed up after two. This guy was either an Ama-Whisperer, or that fine ass had her feeling loquacious.

Or she was under the influence of kitten mind control.

The guy blinked at her for a moment as if processing her words. Would he reprimand her for being careless, like everyone else felt obliged to? Instead, he nodded toward the kitten.

"Listen, if you could go to the other side, that might get it to move so one of us can catch it."

Ama braced a hand on the man's fine, muscular ass—because she could, and who could blame her, and something thumped against the bottom of the truck—to pop to a stand and hurry around to the other side of the truck. Good thing this road was barely traveled. For that matter, good thing she'd been traveling it. Or the guy might be here forever waiting for the kitten to jump into his hands.

She laid down on the other side and *pspsps*'d at the kitten. As the guy had anticipated, the kitten flinched at her universal kitty summons and ran toward him so he could grab it with one large hand and scramble out from under the truck.

Ama skipped back around the truck, excited to see the kitten up close.

Then skidded to a halt. The rest of the man, now standing upright, was as fine as his ass. Tall, blonde, muscular, and gorgeous in a movie Thor—early Avengers; definitely not *End Game* era—kind of way but without the 1980s shoulder pad cape. Instead of Asgardian armor, he wore jeans, work boots, and a dark blue plaid flannel rolled up to his elbows and unbuttoned to show off the plain white t-shirt painted on his ripped torso.

That's a good look. She appreciated to view for a moment before he held out his cupped hands toward her.

"It's more mud than cat." He nodded at the shivering bundle with gold eyes.

She leaned forward for a better peep. Sure enough, the poor thing was soaked and trembling, but not muddy. Its distinctive mottled black-brown-biscuit coat coloration was unmistakable. "Not a black cat. A Tortie." She flashed Thor a triumphant smile before looking at the kitten. "Well, hello there, beautiful. You're in good hands."

Not sure why she said that because she had no idea what manner of hands Thor had. Her guilt at the lie multiplied when he shoved the bundle at her, frowning. "He'd be better off in your hands. You look like someone who could handle a new pet. Or know someone who can."

"She."

He tilted his head as if she spoke Klingon.

"Torties are girls. So, she's a she. Unless she's a he." Which was rare.

"Uh, yeah. That's usually how it works."

Ama shrugged. "Sure, why not."

When he shoved the shivering bundle at her again, she flinched back, waving her hand in front of her. "Oh, no. The cat distribution system chose you."

He frowned at her like she wasn't making sense. A common expression because it was a common occurrence for her. "The cat... what?"

"The cat distribution system. You see, cats are magical creatures crafted in the pits of Mordor that somehow know who most needs their diabolical influence."

He blinked at her "You think I need diabolical influence in my life?"

"Not me. The universe." Ama shrugged and laughed. "Guess it thinks some chaos might be good for you. You can't refuse their offering."

"Ya know, this isn't the one ring to rule them all. I *can* refuse this offering."

She ignored his *Lord of the Rings* reference—who even made them these days?—and grinned at the kitten that had already curled up within the cozy bed of his hands. "Lucky you were just gifted with a tortoiseshell tabby. They're the spawn of Satan and sweet little cherubs. They're two cats in one, like a BOGO of kitty cray-cray. She'll zig when you expect her to zag and you'll hate every minute of it but she'll wrap you around her little paws."

"Maybe I'm just the conduit for the cat distribution system to choose *you* to add some chaos to *your* life." He shoved the kitten, who was already eyes-closed and purring, toward her again.

"*More* chaos?" She wrapped her hands around his and pushed his bundle, hands and all, against his chest and tried to dry the sleepy little bit with the ends of his flannel shirt. "I'm already a chaos tornado stuffed in a hurricane of crazy and wrapped with a blizzard of anarchy."

"Then a cat would be a perfect addition."

Ama shook her head. As much as she'd love to have a pet, she was already responsible for the care and feeding of tiny humans throughout the week. She relished her job at the daycare facility, but adding similar duties to her free time would overtax what little focus she had. Just the thought suddenly exhausted her. She struggled to pull further explanation out. "No way, Thor. You look all big and responsible. Just feed her, water her, give her a cat box, and let her completely rule your life."

"Did you just call me Thor?" His bright blue eyes raked her face as if looking for something. Then he dislodged one hand from the purring bundle and swiped a wet thumb across her cheek "Your, uh, Saturday night clubbing makeup smeared a bit."

His finger was cold, but heat rushed to her face and she ducked her head. Her Saturday night clubbing makeup consisted of neon streaks and splatters from top to bottom. She'd laid down a midnight blue base to better offset the neon so it glowed more brightly in the strobe black lights of the dance floor. The look didn't have quite the same impact on a sunny outdoor roadside location.

Maybe she should dye her hair pink.

All her excitement over the kitten rescue and finding a possible dead body evaporated for no other reason than she'd spent all her spoons on this social interaction. Such was the way of her life, and it severely crimped her social opportunities. She stared at the pavement and tried to think of words that would explain why she was about to turn around and walk straight back to her car.

No words came. But the constriction of social expectation did, because he no doubt expected her to say something, and it clamped on her like a vise. Like it always did when she'd talked too much. She struggled for air and tears burned at the corner of her eye lids. She hated this night-and-day switch her body and mind always did to her. Like she was Dr. Jekyl and Mr. Hyde… if one was a chatty over-sharer of useless information and the other was the worst kind of introvert, incapable of uttering words, period.

"My name's Arkyn. Arkyn Drekison."

Ama was moments from bolting, but Thor's—Arkyn's— calm voice wrapped around her like a hug. Images of soft grass and sloping hills and warm sunshine flashed in her head. The smell of earth and the sound of the life deep within its dirt.

It grounded her. So many people loved the thought of flying among the clouds or bobbing in the waves as if that perceived freedom from the bonds of gravity was somehow a good thing. But Ama felt that untethered sensation every day, as if nothing anchored her to this world, to this life. As if a mere breeze or exhale or whim of Fate would send her drifting into the emptiness of space and away from everything she knew. As it so often had throughout her life.

Toes gripping ground, the firmness, the solidity, of the planet beneath her feet was what she preferred. Like a hug, keeping her from the dark abyss that hovered at the edges of her consciousness.

Arkyn's voice eased the vice around her lungs a bit so she could breathe normally. The heat rolling from his body surrounded her and tied her to the present so she didn't have to fear she might drift away and disappear like early morning mist.

She inhaled deeply, latching on to the last bit of social

strength she had, and gave him a tight smile. "Nice to meet you, Arkyn. I'm Ama Payne. I'm glad you're not dead. Now I need to leave."

She turned and power-walked back to her car. His voice carried to her. "Can I at least get your number. You know, if case I have spawn of Satan questions?"

No way. No way would anything good come of giving him her number. She was whiplash in neon-spattered leggings and chunky heeled platform boots. Any positive karma she'd earned helping the cat distribution system get its man would be negated if she tried to continue a relationship with him, no matter how nice his ass.

Still, she liked being around him. And he'd looked so lost at the thought of taking care of his newfound kitten. She'd be cruel to leave him without any sort of backup.

So Ama slowed as she drove past him, rolled down her passenger window, and shouted her number. There. Her guilt was assuaged and it was up to him to remember it.

Pancake would taste so good right now.

Find "What a Dragon Loves" at your favorite online retailer site: https://books2read.com/WhataDragonLoves

Made in the USA
Columbia, SC
02 August 2024

39854988R00083